P9-DCO-478

Penina Levine

Is a Potato Pancake

Taylor
Pierce
is a Postal Pioneer

Penina Levine

Is a Potato Pancake

Rebecca O'Connell

ILLUSTRATED BY **Majella Lue Sue**

ROARING BROOK PRESS

NEW YORK

NOTE: The story Penina is thinking of in Chapter 19 is "Christmas Every Day"
by William Dean Howells. Thanks to Patte Kelley of Carnegie Library of Pittsburgh
for solving that reference stumper.

Text copyright © 2008 by Rebecca O'Connell
Illustrations copyright © 2008 by Majella Lue Sue

Published by Roaring Brook Press
Roaring Brook Press is a division of Holtzbrinck Publishing
Holdings Limited Partnership
175 Fifth Avenue, New York, New York 10010
www.roaringbrookpress.com

All rights reserved
Distributed in Canada by H. B. Fenn and Company, Ltd.

Library of Congress Cataloging-in-Publication Data
O'Connell, Rebecca, 1968–
Penina Levine is a potato pancake / Rebecca O'Connell ; illustrated by Majella Lue
Sue. — 1st ed.
p. cm.
Summary: When she finds her best friend is going to Aruba for vacation and her
favorite teacher is taking a long leave of absence, sixth-grader Penina is not looking
forward to Hanukkah with her little sister who is always stealing the spotlight.
ISBN-13: 978-1-59643-213-0   ISBN-10: 1-59643-213-6
[1. Hanukkah—Fiction. 2. Sisters—Fiction. 3. Best friends—Fiction. 4. Friendship—
Fiction. 5. Schools—Fiction. 6. Jews—United States—Fiction.]
I. Lue Sue, Majella, ill. II. Title.
PZ7.O2167Pep 2008   [Fic]—dc22   2008011137
Roaring Brook Press books are available for special promotions and premiums. For
details, contact: Director of Special Markets, Holtzbrinck Publishers.

Book design by Jennifer Browne
Printed in the United States of America
First edition October 2008
2   4   6   8   10   9   7   5   3   1

In memory of my grandmothers,

Belle and Rosie

Contents

1. Splat

"No," Penina said, "I think we should wait."

The mountain of Hanukkah gifts was higher than the clock on top of the bookshelves. The presents were shiny and glittery and colorful, and it looked like there were dozens of them, scores, hundreds.

There were presents from Mom and Dad to Penina or Mimsy, presents from Mom to Dad or from Dad to Mom, presents from Mom's students or Dad's principal to the whole Levine family, presents mailed to them from faraway aunts and uncles and cousins, and a little mound of presents for the pet cat, Daisy.

But the presents from Penina weren't in the pile. They weren't ready yet. That was one of the great things about Hanukkah. It lasted eight nights. If you didn't have everything wrapped and ready by the first night, you still had a week to catch up. That's what she'd been hoping, anyway.

"Let's not open them tonight. Let's wait till

Grandma and Grandpa get here. That way, we can do it all together," Penina said. Grandma and Grandpa wouldn't be here for five more days, plenty of time to finish her gifts for Mom and Dad. She was making them coupon books, twelve coupons apiece. "Redeem this coupon for a thorough vacuuming of the den" and "This coupon good for 30 minutes of peace and quiet on the morning of your choice." The coupons were going to be hand-painted in watercolor and bound in poster-board covers with colorful lacing. She thought about running upstairs and finishing them quickly, but that wouldn't work. She was using glitter glue to decorate the covers, and that took a while to dry.

"No, now!" said Mimsy. She shrugged one shoulder and tilted her head, her Cuteness Routine. "Please? Pretty please?"

The Cuteness Routine was a powerful weapon. Penina had nothing to match it.

"I don't see why we can't each open one," Mom said.

"There will still be plenty left to open when your grandparents get here," said Dad. "Let's light the candles first, then we'll open presents."

"Yay!" yelled Mimsy. "Hooray!" She ran around the living room and twirled like a ballerina—a short, clumsy ballerina—in front of all the gifts. "Open mine. Open mine. Open mine," she chanted.

"Take it easy, Mimsykin," said Dad. He held Mimsy's shoulder to keep her from spinning, which Penina thought was like putting his hands between the blades of a rotating fan, but it worked anyway.

"Okay, girls, who will help me light the menorah?" said Mom.

"Me!" yelled Mimsy, and she shot across the room to the front window. That's where Mom had set up the menorah. It was a tall brass candleholder with room for nine candles: one for each night of Hanukkah, plus one helper candle, the *shamash*. The wrapped packages were shiny, but the polished menorah was radiant, luminous, brilliant.

"I get to pick the candles!" screamed Mimsy. She was already digging through the box. "I want pink and purple!"

Why did Mimsy get to pick the candles? Shouldn't Penina get first pick? She was older, so it was only fair that she should go first. But if Mimsy picked two candles tonight (one for the first night, plus the *shamash*), then tomorrow Penina could pick three. They'd take turns night to night, and on the last night, Penina would get to fill the whole menorah, nine candles, all by herself.

"Okay, Mimsy," Penina said, "you pick tonight. I'll pick tomorrow."

"That's fair," said Mom. She took the candles from Mimsy and placed them in the menorah.

"No! The purple one is the *shamash!*" Mimsy screamed.

Mom reversed the candles. "Okay, ready?" she asked. Mom sang the first note of the blessing herself, then everyone joined in.

Baruch ata Adonai

As they sang the blessing, Mom lit a match and held it to the purple *shamash* candle. She shook out the match and took the *shamash* out of the menorah. She used the shamash to light the pink candle, the candle for the first night.

le-hadlik ner

Shel Hanukkah.

When Penina sang "*shel Hanukkah,*" she always thought of a smooth pink seashell, but that's not what the blessing meant. It was really a way of giving thanks for the candle-lighting tradition.

"*Hanukkah sameach,*" said Dad, which was Hebrew for *happy Hanukkah.* He gave Penina and Mimsy a squeeze, but Penina had to shrug out of it because Mimsy was jumping up and down, and it was jolting her.

"You said we could open presents!" Mimsy yelled.

Penina didn't have anything to give Mom and Dad.

Well, she did, but her gifts weren't finished. She wished she'd gotten the coupon books done earlier. She wished she'd just bought her parents something at the mall. "I don't think we should open presents tonight," she said.

"Sure we should," said Mom.

"Just one apiece," said Dad.

"Pina!" yelled Mimsy, as if she knew Penina was joking about not opening presents.

Penina was not joking. She didn't have anything to give her parents—or Mimsy, come to think of it—and that was no joke.

"Hanukkah is not about presents," Penina declared. "It's not about malls and catalogs. It's about—"

Mom interrupted. "It's about guerilla warfare." She gave a flat little laugh. "But that doesn't mean we can't have presents."

Technically, Mom was right. Hanukkah was about guerilla warfare—sneak attacks and hand-to-hand fighting. It was about the Maccabees' victory for religious freedom. It was about—

"Open mine! Open mine!" Mimsy screamed, swinging two blue tubes like battle axes. "They're for you! I made them!"

"Okay," said Mom. She took a tube from Mimsy. "Daddy and I will open these. You girls each pick one to open tonight."

Penina couldn't believe the greed of these people. Hanukkah wasn't just about opening gifts. It was the celebration of the rededication of the Temple. Mrs. Greenbaum had been over it with them in religious school a thousand times. In ancient Judea, the evil

King Antiochus had banned Judaism. He wrecked the Jewish Temple, and anyone caught being Jewish was killed.

Judah Maccabee and his brothers fought Antiochus, even though Antiochus had a huge army and all the Maccabees had were sticks and stones. Miraculously, the Maccabees won. They had a big celebration to rededicate the Temple. *That's* what Hanukkah was about, not presents.

"Hanukkah doesn't have anything to do with presents," Penina shouted. "Why can't you think about the true meaning of Hanukkah?"

"Don't you want your presents, Penina?" asked Mom. "Last week you had a long list of things you wanted for Hanukkah. What's gotten into you?

"Nothing," Penina answered.

"You know, Pen," Dad mentioned offhandedly, as if he weren't about to rev up into Lecture Mode, which Penina could tell he was, "exchanging gifts has been an important part of celebrating Hanukkah for hundreds of years."

Penina gave him a skeptical look.

"Really," said Dad. "Hanukkah was traditionally a time for European Jews to pay the teachers in the community. The students brought *gelt*—money—to school to give the teachers at Hanukkah. That's where we get the tradition of Hanukkah gifts."

"Especially for teachers," Mom said, grinning. She was a teacher. So was Dad.

But I don't have anything to give you. Penina was all set to admit it, to explain that their gifts would be done by the eighth night but weren't ready yet. Her parents would understand, and when they got the coupon books, they'd see it had been worth the wait. Penina was just opening her mouth to tell them, but Mimsy opened hers first.

"Here! Take this! Mine first! Mine first!"

"Okay, Mimsy," said Mom. She picked the tape off one end of the tube of wrapping paper and slid out another paper tube. She unrolled the inside tube and gasped. "Oh, Mimsy, thank you! A painting! It's just beautiful! Oh, look! This is just exquisite! Thank you!" She hugged Mimsy and gave her a big, loud kiss.

Dad tore the wrapping off his present and made a big huge fuss over the painting from Mimsy. "Thank you, Mimsy! This is fantastic! Look at your use of color and line! Wow! Some of my students don't produce work like that."

Dad's students were teenagers. Dad taught high school art. There was no way Mimsy's painting was as good as a high school student's. Dad didn't know what he was talking about.

"Pick out your gifts, girls—one each," said Mom.

Mimsy picked up a flat square box, but it wasn't from her pile of gifts. It was from Penina's. "Open this, Pina," she said.

Penina's gift for Mimsy was really nice. It was a stuffed toy cat with white and yellow patches, just like their pet cat, Daisy. It was life-sized and extra soft, and it was on a shelf in the bookstore at the mall. Penina had picked it out and put aside the money for it. She just hadn't gotten it yet.

"Open it. Open it. I made it at school," said Mimsy. She thought play group was school.

Penina took off the curly silver ribbon and the glossy blue wrapping and the top lid of the box. It was a paper plate. It was the outside of a paper plate, with the inside cut out and all kinds of junk glued to the rim.

"This is a button, and this is a flower, and this is a piece of yarn," Mimsy yelled. She took the plate from Penina and held it up to her own face. "It's a picture frame, see?"

"Thanks, Mimsy," said Penina. "It's really nice."

"It's beautiful, honey," said Mom.

"It's a really special gift," said Dad. "What a nice thing to make for your sister."

"And I glued on a pinecone right here, see?" said Mimsy.

9

"It's great, Mimsy. Thanks," Penina said. She put the paper-plate frame back in the box, but before she could put the lid back on, Mimsy grabbed the plate back.

"And these are beads. This one is orange, and this one is red."

"Okay, very nice. Thanks for the frame," said Penina. Mimsy should have just kept the thing if she liked it that much.

"And this one is blue, and this one is orange like that one—"

"Okay! I see it. It's wonderful. I said thank you. Do I have to say it again? Fine. *Thank you!*" Penina yelled. She shouted. She screamed so hard she thought she saw the Hanukkah lights flicker.

Mimsy started to cry.

Dad picked her up and rocked her. Mom plopped down on the couch and put her face in her hands.

"You know what, Penina?" said Mom. "I am really tired of hearing you yell at your sister. She's seven years younger than you are. Why can't you just be nice to her?"

"Why can't she be nice to me?" Penina answered. The words were out before she had time to think about them.

"She was nice to you. She gave you a handcrafted present."

Mimsy lifted her head from Dad's soaking-wet shoulder. "I *made* it for her!" she wailed. She sniffed twice and put her head back down.

"And I said thank you. Come on. I said it a hundred times, but she just wouldn't quit bragging about it," Penina said. She hated that stupid frame. She hated Hanukkah presents. She hated Hanukkah.

"You know what I want for Hanukkah?" said Mom. She'd taken her face out of her hands but was still slumped in the corner of the couch. "Penina, I want you to be nice to your sister, for the full eight days."

"I am nice to her!" Penina shouted. This was so unfair. How could she be nice when Mimsy was such a brat?

Dad sat down next to Mom. Mimsy snuggled in his lap. "Your mother is asking you not to overreact.

If you have a problem with your sister, talk to her."

Mom held out her hand, as if she wanted Penina to take it. Penina decided not to notice. She was not in a hand-holding mood. "I know you get frustrated," Mom said, "but you're the big sister. You have a responsibility to behave like one."

Mimsy turned to Penina and smiled. Mimsy had snot on her face, and her curly hair was frizzed out all over the place. How anyone could think she was cute was a mystery to Penina.

Mom cleared her throat and said, "My parents are coming in a few days, and I don't want them to see you fighting with your sister. Please, as my Hanukkah present, would you just *cool it?*"

Penina didn't answer. She didn't look at Mom and Dad and Mimsy. She looked at the menorah instead, and as she watched, pink and purple wax dropped off the candles, onto the base of the menorah.

Splat.

2. What's So Funny?

Penina's toes were frozen solid. Everything else was drippy: her scarf, her boots, her nose. She found a tissue in her coat pocket and swiped at the drippiness.

She felt herself thawing out. The snow melted off her coat and went *drip, drip, drip* on the floor of her locker. She arranged it so the drops from her coat fell beside her boots, not in them.

"Ready?" Zozo asked. She had her coat off, books out, shoes on. No boots, no drips, no frozen nose or toes. Only a few snowflakes in her hair and the pink glow on her cheekbones showed she'd been out in the cold all morning.

"Almost. I have to put on my shoes," Penina said. She unzipped her backpack and got out . . .

Nothing. Her shoes weren't there. She had her lunch, her take-home folder, her Language Arts book, strawberry-banana lip balm, pencils, pens, erasers, a green plastic comb, a Band-Aid, and $1.97 in change, but not her shoes.

"Oh, shoot!" said Penina. "I forgot my shoes."

"Call your mom and have her bring them," said Zozo.

"I don't know," Penina said. Which was worse: walking around in heavy, wet, bright green winter boots or getting the lecture about responsibility?

Penina put her feet back in her boots. They were cold and squishy on the inside and wet and snowy on the outside. The snow was stuck deep in the treads, and a little bit melted off with every step. She left a trail of drippy footprints from the hallway to her desk.

"It is so cold. I practically have frostbite!" said Ryan. He sat behind Penina and over one row, right behind Zozo. "See?" He put his fingers on Zozo's wrist. "Ice cold!"

Zozo moved her wrist and covered it with her sleeve. "Yes, Ryan, your fingers are very cold," she said. She said it like she was the babysitter and Ryan was the pesky preschooler.

"I had to wait for the bus for half an hour," said Ryan.

So what? It took Penina and Zozo at least that long to walk to school. "But you got to warm up on the school bus," Penina called, past Zozo and back to Ryan. "We had to freeze the whole way to school."

Ryan looked at Penina like *I was talking to Zozo, not to you.* Penina got that look all the time.

Penina wiggled her toes and felt the water swish around inside her boots. At least it was warm water now. She could feel her feet getting pruney. She'd have to ask Mrs. Brown if she could call home. Cell phones were not allowed to be on at school. If Penina wanted to call her mom, she'd have to ask to go to the office, preferably before the homeroom bell. She got up and squelched in her boots to Mrs. Brown's desk at the front of the room.

"Mrs. Brown, I need to—" Penina stopped. Mrs. Brown didn't look right. Her nose was pink, but not out-in-the-cold pink; more like trying-not-to-cry pink. Her eyes were pink, too, and everything—her hair, her face, her shoulders—looked droopy.

"Yes, Penina? What do you need?" Mrs. Brown said. She smiled, but it was the worst smile Penina had ever seen. She looked like one of those sad clowns, but without the beard stubble and the smashed hat.

"Nothing. I just, um . . ." Penina hated to bother Mrs. Brown if she was in the middle of trying not to cry. She knew how it felt. The more you tried, the worse it got, and someone was always right there, going, "What's wrong? Are you okay? Why are you crying?" That didn't help at all.

"It's okay, Penina," Mrs. Brown said. She gave another horrible sad-clown smile. "I got some bad news this morning, but I'll be all right." She smiled again. This one was better, with teeth and crinkly eyes. "I'm sorry if I scared you. Now, what were you going to ask?"

What's wrong? Are you okay? Why are you crying? That's all Penina could think about asking. "Can I help?" she whispered, and it surprised her, because she had been planning to ask about using the phone.

"Oh, no. But thank you. Thanks for asking," said Mrs. Brown. She straightened a stack of papers on her desk, leafed through her attendance notebook.

Penina rocked gently from foot to foot. Her boots made watery noises.

Mrs. Brown came around her big desk and looked at Penina's feet. "Did you forget your shoes?" she asked.

"Yes," Penina admitted.

"With me it's umbrellas. I've left umbrellas in restaurants and waiting rooms all over this town."

Penina nodded. Actually, she had a hard time with umbrellas, too.

"Would you like to call home and ask someone to bring your shoes to you?"

"Yes, please."

"Here you go." Mrs. Brown handed Penina the hall pass. They looked at the hall pass, looked at each other, and they both let out loud, snorky laughs.

It was a chicken, a yellowy-pink rubber chicken with *hall pass* written on the belly in permanent ink. It had always been a chicken, since the beginning of the year at least. Penina had used the chicken hall pass a hundred times before, but it had never seemed funny until that very moment. A chicken! The hall pass was a chicken! Other classes had laminated cards that said *pass*, but Mrs. Brown's class had poultry.

Mrs. Brown really was crying now, and Penina was too. It was the laughing kind of crying, with tears and sniffles and gasps. Penina looked back at Zozo, and Zozo gave Penina a look like, *What's so funny?*

Penina picked up the chicken's three-toed foot and made it wave at Zozo. Zozo smiled like, *Well, I don't get it, but I'm glad you're happy.*

"I'll be right back," Penina told Mrs. Brown, and she splashed down the hall in her soggy boots.

3. A Bunch of Idiots

"Pina! You forgot your shoes!" yelled Mimsy, and she skipped across the classroom, swinging Penina's shoes in a white plastic grocery bag.

Everyone in the whole entire class, except for Zozo and most of the boys, went crazy.

"She's so cute!"

"Look at her!"

"Like a doll!"

"Penina, your sister is just adorable!"

The good news: Penina could finally take off her wet boots. The bad news: her classmates were a bunch of idiots.

"She's so sweet!"

"Have you ever seen such curly hair?"

"Mimsy, come here. Can I give you a hug?"

Mimsy would have walked right past Penina to go give that stupid girl a hug, but Penina grabbed her as she went by.

"Thanks for the shoes, Mimsy," Penina said. She took the bag from Mimsy. "Good-bye."

"And socks, too," Mimsy answered. "I bringed you your fish socks."

"Brought," Penina said. It made her sick. Mimsy knew how to speak English. The baby talk was an act, totally fake.

Where was Mom? Mimsy hadn't driven here herself. Mom was probably in the office, having coffee with Mrs. Mulrane while Mimsy took over the class.

"How old are you, Mimsy?" asked someone a couple of rows back, probably Anne or Suzie, but Penina wasn't sure. She didn't turn around to see.

"Four," said Mimsy. She held up four fingers, just in case any of the sixth graders whose math class she was interrupting didn't know what four meant.

"Wow. You're a big girl!" said Anne. It was

definitely Anne. Penina recognized her voice. What was wrong with her? She had her own little sisters. One of them was a baby. Didn't Anne get enough cutie-cuteness at home?

"Are you getting ready for Santa Claus?" Anne asked.

"No!" Mimsy yelled, and giggled and dimpled and spun around.

"No? Why not?" said Anne, Mimsy's new best friend.

"There's no such thing as Santa Claus!" yelled Mimsy. You could tell she thought Anne was very silly for even bringing it up.

Everyone in the whole entire class, even Zozo and most of the boys, gasped. Then they started shouting.

"What?"

"Don't say that!"

"Of course there is!"

"Penina, why doesn't your sister believe in Santa?"

Penina raised her hand. "Mrs. Brown, may I go to my locker and change into my shoes? I'll walk Mimsy back out on the way."

Mrs. Brown opened her mouth, but she didn't have a chance to answer before Mimsy's fan club started protesting.

"Not yet!"

"Let her stay!"

"She's not bothering anybody."

"Penina, your sister can wait here."

Penina stood up in her wet boots. She thought about grabbing Mimsy by the arm, but she stopped herself. Instead, she put her hand out for Mimsy to take.

Mimsy ignored the hand. "I made you a present, Pina," she shouted. "It's in the bag with your shoes!"

"Okay. Come on. Let's go."

"Look!" Mimsy shouted. She took back the bag and pulled out a piece of paper with scribbles all over it. "This is me, and this is you, and this is Daisy, chasing a ball of yarn."

"Aww!" said every single person in the entire room. If Mimsy didn't get out of here soon, the whole class was going to die of adorableness poisoning.

Thank goodness, Zozo was immune. She'd seen too much of Mimsy to think she was cute. She gave Penina a sympathetic look. Mrs. Brown might be immune, too. While everyone else was cooing and drooling and trying to pat Mimsy's curls, Mrs. Brown was waiting for Mimsy to stop chattering. She tapped her toes, tapped her marker on the whiteboard, tapped her fingers on her desk. "Thank you, Mimsy," she finally said, "I'm sure Penina appreciates the shoes and the picture. Have a nice afternoon."

"Okay!" Mimsy yelled, and she disappeared— with Penina's shoes—into her crowd of admirers. A group of girls had gotten up to ooh and ahh over Mimsy.

"Anne, Jackie, Suzie, please take your seats," Mrs. Brown said. She wasn't the kind of teacher who yelled. She might give extra homework or a pop quiz, but she was never mean.

The worst thing she'd ever done was cancel Costume Day, but that was because someone had dug big holes out of the bulletin board and no one would say who had done it. Penina didn't know, otherwise she might have told—anonymously. She'd been looking forward to Costume Day. She and Zozo were going to be Jane Goodall and Dian Fossey, the famous scientists. They'd worn the costumes at home, but it wasn't the same.

So Mrs. Brown didn't yell at the girls to sit down, but you could tell she really wanted them to sit.

They sat.

Penina took the shoe bag in one hand and Mimsy's wrist in the other and sloshed in her boots toward the hallway. She didn't take the chicken pass.

Her hands were full, and besides, she didn't want to bother Mrs. Brown.

Mrs. Brown, the sad-faced clown, thought Penina. It was a nice rhyme, but it was a terrible nickname.

"Bye, Mimsy," sang Mimsy's loyal fans.

Mimsy paused to blow kisses, and the girls sighed and squealed and smiled so much Penina thought they were going to wet their pants.

"Come on!" she said to Mimsy and dragged her out the door.

Penina's soaking socks were molded to her toes. It wasn't that bad. She could have lasted through the day with wet feet. It would have been better than this nightmare visit from Mimsy. Next time, she'd see if there were any dry shoes in the lost-and-found. Even just socks. Even just flip-flops.

"Bye-bye, Mimsy, bye-bye," the class called after them.

Penina's waterlogged steps in the empty hallway were very noisy, but she could still hear Mrs. Brown's voice. "Put away your books and take out a clean sheet of paper. We're going to have a pop quiz."

4. Powers

"Seven out of ten, but we hadn't even gone over half the stuff on the quiz. We only just started the chapter this morning." Penina took a carrot stick and bit it in half with one chomp.

"Well, study hard, and you'll do fine on the next one," Mom said. She put some carrot and celery sticks on Mimsy's plate.

Mimsy took them off and stacked them up on the table. Penina wasn't allowed to play with her food, but when Mimsy did it, nobody said a word.

"Hey, Mimsy, you made a pyramid—great!" said Dad.

Correction: nobody said a word unless it was to praise Mimsy's budding gift for architecture.

"Can you do it with four sticks on the bottom now?" Dad asked, and he and Mimsy got started on a vegetable version of the Valley of Kings, with carrot-and-celery monuments rising between their plates. Mom arranged rolls in the shape of the Great Sphinx.

Hadn't Penina been talking about her schoolwork? Wasn't that an important topic? "Guess what we're doing in math class," Penina said. She had to put a lot of force behind her words to be heard over the big construction project. "Powers!"

Dad looked up from his work. "You mean, like, the power of strength, the power of invisibility?"

"The power to cloud men's minds," said Mom, in a deep, mysterious voice.

"Princess power!" yelled Mimsy. She did some kind of power move, and the veggie pyramids all fell over.

"No, *powers*," Penina said. "Like, two *to the power* of three is two times two times two."

"The power to topple megalithic structures!" said Mom, scooping up the scattered celery and carrot sticks. The roll-Sphinx was still standing.

"The power to leap tall buildings in a single bound!" said Dad. He made his hand be a superhero, leaping over the napkin holder, snatching the Sphinx's head, and flying it to Dad's mouth, where he bit it in half.

The power to finish telling my parents about my day, the power to get them to listen to me about anything at all, ever. Now that would be an amazing power.

Penina leaned back so she could look out of the kitchen, into the living room, and at the menorah in the front window. Three candles tonight. One for the first night, one for the second night, one for the *shamash*. Orange and yellow and white—Penina had picked them to match the colors in Daisy's coat. Not that anyone noticed. Not that anyone asked.

"It's eight, by the way," Penina said. She stood her fork up in her potato. She didn't really like baked potatoes, but they were fun to stab.

"Be nice to your potato, Penina," said Mom.

"No, it's only six fifteen," said Dad.

Penina took her fork out of her potato and stuck it in her meatloaf—turkey loaf, really. It wasn't bad. The trick was to know it was turkey. If your mouth expected a meatloaf taste, you were disappointed, but if you got in the mood for something that wasn't even made of beef, turkey loaf tasted pretty good. "Not eight o'clock, the number eight. Two to the third power is eight," Penina explained.

"She's right!" Mom exclaimed. She didn't have to sound so surprised.

"She doesn't get that from my side of the family," said Dad.

It was a sort of family legend that Dad was

helpless at math and Mom couldn't do drawing or painting of any kind, like Jack Sprat and his wife. Penina privately recited,

> *Penina's Dad*
> *Could not add.*
> *His wife could do no art.*
> *And so they sorted out the work*
> *And each one did a part.*

It wasn't strictly true. Dad could convert centimeters to inches without even thinking about it, and Mom doodled cartoon fish and dolphins and octopuses all over everything.

"Well, Penina, it's nice to know I gave you *something*," said Mom. It was another family joke. According to relatives, friends, and random strangers at the mall, Penina and Mimsy looked a lot like Dad. "They sprang fully formed from the head of their father," Mom liked to say, when anyone brought up the Levine family resemblance. "I had nothing to do with it."

This legend, like the Levine-Sprat legend, was only a little bit true. Sure, Penina and Mimsy and Dad all had brown eyes and dark curly hair, but they weren't clones. Penina didn't have Dad's and Mimsy's dimples. Mimsy and Penina didn't have Dad's bushy eyebrows.

Dad smiled at Mom and Penina. "My math mavens," he said. "My marvelous math mavens."

"I'm a math maiden!" yelled Mimsy. "I can count backward!" And she did, from ten down to "blast off," which wasn't technically a number, but it was still an extremely impressive bit of performance math, even if she did skip six and get five and four reversed.

Mom and Dad clapped. Penina got up and put her plate—potato and all—in the sink. "May I be excused? I have a ton of homework."

"Oh, Penina," said Mom, "I'm so glad you've started powers. Next it's square roots and cube roots and then, *imaginary numbers!*" She said *imaginary numbers* the way another mom might say *chocolate chip cookies!*

Hot-air balloon rides!

Sapphires and emeralds!

Penina sat back down. "Imaginary numbers?"

Mom grabbed a couple of pencils and the notebook they used for phone messages. She sat down next to Penina and wrote

$$2^2=4$$

"Two to the power of two is four. Two squared is

four," Mom said. "So the *square root* of four is two."

Penina nodded. It made sense. It made beautiful sense. She took the pencil out of her mouth and did a page full of squares and square roots. She went up to **12 √144** and back down to 1.

"The square root of one is one. It has to be!" Penina said. She really was a math wiz. She was Thomas Edison, Marie Curie, Harry Potter.

"That's absolutely right," said Mom. She squeezed Penina's shoulders, smoothed Penina's hair. Dad and Mimsy were gone. The dinner dishes were cleared. It was only Mom and Penina, their square pages of square roots, and the distant glow of the Hanukkah candles.

"Okay," said Mom, all back to serious mathematical business. "If one is the square root of one, then what is the square root of *negative* one?"

"It's got to be negative one," Penina guessed.

"No!" shouted Mom, and Penina wondered if fun times in Mathland were over, but Mom wasn't angry, just emphatic. "A negative times a negative always equals a positive. Trust me on this. There's a way to prove it, but it's complicated."

"That's all right. I believe you."

"Good," said Mom, "So, how do you get the square root of negative one?"

Penina concentrated on the square root of negative one. It made her stomach feel queasy. "I don't know," Penina said. She took a piece of paper and wrote

$$\sqrt{-1} \ \sqrt{-1} \ \sqrt{-1} \ \sqrt{-1} \ \sqrt{-1}$$

all over it.

"It's imaginary," whispered Mom. She wrote

i1

on a new piece of paper.

There was a whole universe of imaginary numbers. And mathematicians used them. All the time.

Penina couldn't believe it. It was like living in Oz.

Mom told Penina about Gerolamo Cardano, a famous mathematician who had discovered imaginary numbers hundreds of years ago. She told Penina how imaginary numbers were used in physics and medicine. Mom told her about Ms. Ober, her own high school algebra teacher, and how inspirational she had been.

"That's like Mrs. Brown," Penina said.

"That's good," said Mom. "You'll always remember Mrs. Brown."

"Uh-huh," said Penina. She knew she always would remember Mrs. Brown, but she'd probably remember her more for the chicken hall pass than for anything to do with powers or square roots or imaginary numbers.

5. Pretty Twisted

"Imaginary numbers! They can't exist. They're impossible, but they *have* to exist—at least on paper—otherwise how could you explain the square root of negative numbers?" The wonder of it boggled Penina's mind. She thought it should boggle Zozo's mind, too, but Zozo didn't look boggled.

"Do you have your shoes today?" she said.

"Yes, plus a backup pair. I'm going to keep my sneakers at school from now on." Plus extra socks, plus a towel in case her feet got wet, plus a little gym bag to keep everything in in her locker. The little gym bag was new, last night's Hanukkah present from Mom and Dad. Penina had to admire their timing.

"Good, because I got a nine on that quiz. It's the only point I've missed all year."

"Oh," said Penina. She knew what Zozo was getting at, but she didn't know what to say about it. She leaned against their neighbor's fence and scraped all the snow off of it as they walked by.

34

"If it weren't for that quiz," said Zozo, "I'd have a perfect math score, and if it weren't for the big fuss over Mimsy, we wouldn't have had that quiz, and if it weren't for Mimsy being in our school, they wouldn't have made a big fuss over her, and if it weren't for you forgetting your shoes, Mimsy would not have been in our school in the first place."

"Maybe Mrs. Brown will let you make up the point," Penina said. It was cold enough to see her breath, and she watched it float past her face as she talked. She and Zozo used to pretend they were dragons with fire breath. They were too old for that now, so Penina pretended to light a cigarette and blow smoke rings.

"My mom really can blow smoke rings," said Zozo. "She's going to teach me how when I'm twenty-one."

It figured. Mrs. Miller would know how to blow smoke rings. She was not a normal mother. She was more like a mother from some alternate universe where children pick their parents, where mothers set up ice-cream-sundae bars for dinner, where negative numbers have actual square roots. "But, Zozo, your mom doesn't smoke."

"Not in fifteen years. Not since she married my dad." Zozo did a quick sideways glance at Penina. Penina did one back. Zozo hardly ever mentioned

35

her father. He died when Zozo was a baby. Penina never knew what to say to Zozo when the subject of fathers came up.

"She quit when she got married?"

"Yes, my dad said the only wedding gift he wanted was for her to quit smoking. He said she needed to stay healthy because he loved her so much, he wanted them to be together for a long, long time."

Wow. That was so romantic. That was so sad. Poor Mrs. Miller. Poor Zozo. Penina's eyes felt a little teary. She put out her mitten to touch her friend.

"Pretty twisted, huh?" Zozo said. No tears here, not even a catch in her voice. "*She's* the smoker, and *he's* the one who dies?"

"Just goes to show," Penina said. Show what? Penina had no idea.

"So, what do you mean, make up the point? Like, extra credit?" Zozo said.

Penina had been imagining the conversation she was going to have with Mrs. Brown that morning.

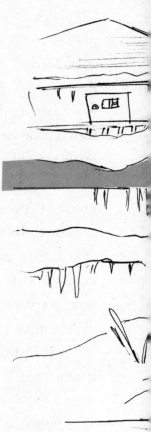

She would ask for the pass and casually bring up the idea of negative numbers having square roots. Mrs. Brown would tell Penina it could be done with imaginary numbers, and Penina would tell Mrs. Brown everything she'd gone over with Mom last night. Mrs. Brown would congratulate Penina on being familiar with lessons from advanced Algebra. She'd give Penina the chicken pass to spend Math period in the library, since Penina had already mastered this chapter.

"Why don't you tell Mrs. Brown that you already know about imaginary numbers? She'll give you extra credit for that." Zozo was her best friend. Zozo was practically an orphan. Penina didn't mind sharing the imaginary numbers talk with Zozo.

"Yeah, not going to happen," Zozo said.

Penina whacked a sign post so the snow slid off the "One Way" arrow onto the sidewalk. *Plop.* That was satisfying.

And so was getting to school before the late bell, tucking her things into her locker, and changing from her snowy boots into warm, dry socks and shoes. Penina tightened her shoelaces and made neat double bows. She was off to a good start. Today was going to be a nice day.

"Oh, no!"

"What's the principal doing here?"

"Where is Mrs. Brown?"

The groans and questions came from Penina's classroom. She and Zozo slammed their lockers and ran in to see what was going on.

6. As Bald as Frosty

"Walk, please. Save running for the gymnasium or for public office," said Dr. Tobin. He was the principal of the school, and he was as bald as Frosty the Snowman. He was taller, though. He kept his neck out and his shoulders up, as if he were constantly ducking under something. He probably was—doorways, banners, low power lines. There are lots of things to bang into when you are Dr. Tobin's height.

"What's with the principal being in our room?" whispered Zozo to Penina.

That was a change. Zozo usually knew all the breaking news. The only reason Penina ever knew anything was that Zozo kept her informed.

Penina shrugged. She had no idea why Dr. Tobin was in their classroom or where Mrs. Brown was or how Zozo expected her to have any better info than anybody else.

"Mrs. Brown asked me to speak with you today,"

Dr. Tobin said. He had a very deep voice, like the lowest note on a double bassoon. "What I have to tell you is not easy to say, and it is not easy to hear, but you are sixth graders, and Mrs. Brown and I agree that you have the requisite level of maturity to assimilate this information."

Penina bit her pencil. She liked crunching into a smooth new pencil, feeling her teeth make dents in the wood. She saw Zozo watching her, and she took the pencil out of her mouth. Zozo thought pencil biting was gross.

"Mrs. Brown is absent today," said Dr. Tobin. "You will have a substitute teacher today and tomorrow. Mrs. Brown will come back to finish the term, but she will not return in January. She has a family emergency and must take an extended leave of absence."

An extended leave of absence. Penina let out a long breath. Whew. That wasn't so bad. Dr. Tobin was making it sound all tragic, like once winter vacation came, they'd never see Mrs. Brown again. But people were *absent* all the time. Then they came back. No big deal.

"When will she be back?" asked Jackie. Penina twisted around to look at her. She looked younger, as if the third-grade Jackie had somehow come and taken her seat. And she was blinking a lot.

"She'll be back on Thursday," said Dr. Tobin. He pulled Mrs. Brown's desk chair out to the front of the room and folded himself up to sit on it. "She'll finish the week here. When you come back from winter vacation, you'll have a new teacher."

Penina put her pencil in her mouth and got in

one deep bite before she saw Zozo looking at her. She put the pencil back on her desk.

"Well, I guess it's 'good-bye, Mrs. Brown,'" whispered Zozo. "I wonder what the new teacher is going to be like. I hope it's someone who never heard of pop quizzes."

Zozo shouldn't say that. Penina scowled at her. Then she raised her hand and asked, "Dr. Tobin, how long will Mrs. Brown's leave of absence be?"

Dr. Tobin let his elbows rest on his knees. He stared at the floor between his feet. The top of his smooth pink head reflected the overhead lights. It would have been funny if the whole thing weren't making Penina completely sick. "Following winter vacation," said the principal, "Mrs. Brown's leave of absence will extend for an indefinite period. She is not expected to return for the foreseeable future."

"She's not coming back," said Zozo. Penina imagined herself kicking Zozo's chair out from under her, ordering her to take that back, daring her to repeat it.

"Yes, she is," Penina answered, without attacking Zozo, without even raising her voice very much. "She's coming back on Thursday, and that means we have only two days to figure out a way to get her to change her mind!"

7. The Yummiest Snack in the World

"Hi, honey. How was school today?" Mom pulled off Penina's hat and shook the snow off of it while Penina took off her boots.

"Fine." Penina shrugged off her coat, and it landed in a snowy heap by the door.

"You're not allowed to leave that there," said Mimsy. "Mom! Pina left her coat on the floor!" She yelled as if their mother were half a mile—instead of two steps—away.

"Pick up your coat, please," Mom instructed.

"I was about to do it. Can't I even have one second to take off my gloves before everyone starts ordering me around?" Penina grabbed her coat and slapped it onto a hook in the closet. The sweatshirt that was already on the hook fell off when she did that, but that wasn't Penina's problem. "The coat is up, okay? Are there any other household chores you would like me to do? Should I polish the floor? Scrub the toilets?"

"Toilets!" shrieked Mimsy, and rolled around giggling her head off.

"That won't be necessary, Penina," said Mom. She put her hand on Penina's back. "Come into the kitchen. Maybe some food will improve your mood."

No, maybe people giving her half a second to hang up her coat before they start yelling at her would improve her mood. But she was kind of hungry. She wouldn't mind a quick snack. "Can I have a pizza muffin?"

Well, no. It turned out she couldn't have a pizza muffin. They were out of English muffins. She could have apples and peanut butter, but only with that natural organic peanut butter that Penina hated. She couldn't have cookies because they weren't "a growing food," and she couldn't have Pop-Tarts because Mom was mad at the company that made them. She could have yogurt, which was gross, or cheese cubes, which she was sick of because she'd had them for lunch, or celery with peanut butter, but it still would be the disgusting kind of peanut butter, so Penina said forget it.

"Fine!" said Mom. "You make your own snack. No cookies or candy or anything like that. As long as it isn't chips of lead paint, I don't care what you eat."

She took Mimsy and left. Penina sat and watched the kitchen door swing shut behind her mother. When the door swung back open a second later, her mother was behind it. "And be sure you clean up after yourself," she said. The door shut. The door opened. "And don't burn anything," said Mom. Then the door swung shut again.

Penina watched the door. Once it had stayed shut for five full seconds, she got up and looked in the fridge. It was full of gross food, food that needed hours of preparation, and food she'd already had for lunch. She was going to starve to death.

Zozo always had fantastic snacks. She had a zillion food allergies, so her mother made her special allergy-free treats. She was probably next door right now, eating corn chips with honey-lime salsa, carob bars, and amazing apple-cinnamon-millet muffins.

Zozo answered on the first ring. "Hi, Penina," she said.

"Hi, Zozo," said Penina, waving to her through the window. Penina's dining room window faced Zozo's living room window, and they liked to talk on the phone watching each other. It was like having a giant videophone. They called it the Window Phone.

"So, what are you doing?" Penina asked.

"Nothing. What are you doing?"

"Nothing."

They went back and forth like that for a while. Zozo's "nothing" turned out to be trying on clothes, deciding what to wear to that year's Christmas parties, and making a list of things she would need to get to complete her outfits.

She'd already had her snack: vegetarian sushi.

"What'd you have?"

"Nothing. All we have is, like, marmalade and green olives." Two foods that lived in the fridge eternally, perpetually, forever and ever, because no one was ever going to eat them, and they never seemed to rot.

"Mmm. Delish. I'll be right over."

It turned out Zozo was kidding about the "delish" part, but not the part about being right over. Seventy-two seconds later, Zozo was in Penina's kitchen.

Well, most of her was in Penina's kitchen. Her head, shoulders, and right arm were in the pantry. "Hey! Canned pineapple! We can make piña colada fritters. Do you have any shredded coconut? Oh wait, never mind, here it is."

Zozo brought an armload of cans, boxes, and bottles to the counter: pineapple, shredded coconut, cornmeal, olive oil, ginger, a tall blue box of salt, and a red-and-white can that had been standing at the very back of the pantry for as long as Penina could remember. "Do you have any eggs?" Zozo asked.

Penina didn't answer. Zozo was pulling the egg carton out of the fridge before she'd finished asking the question. Instead, Penina asked Zozo a question. "What are piña colada fritters?"

"Only the yummiest snack in the world," said Zozo.

And she wasn't kidding. The fritters were crunchy, greasy, sweet and spicy, hot lumps of fried batter studded with pineapple bits and sprinkled with shredded coconut. They were like tropical funnel cakes or flat Hawaiian doughnut holes. "They're like pineapple-coconut latkes," said Penina, once she'd eaten her third.

"*What*-kes?" asked Zozo. She had fritter oil all around her mouth, but only for a second. She took a napkin and wiped her face, then took another one and tossed it to Penina.

Penina wiped her mouth, her hands, the table around her plate. Everything had tiny beads of oil all over it. "Latkes. They're potato pancakes. They're for Hanukkah. You know, because of the miracle of the oil?"

Zozo nodded and took another fritter. Penina supposed Zozo knew the general idea of the Hanukkah story, even if she wasn't quite clear on the details. It was the same way with Penina and Epiphany. She got that Epiphany was the twelfth day of Christmas, but she wasn't 100 percent sure what that meant.

Zozo guessed, "There was only enough oil for one night, but it burned for eight, right?"

"Yup." The Maccabees won back the Temple, but in order to rededicate it, they needed oil for the menorah. It was a special, sacred oil, and there wasn't enough of it. The small amount of oil they had should have burned out after one night, but, miraculously, it kept on burning.

That's how Mrs. Greenbaum told it. Every year, all the religious-school classes had a big latke-fest in the temple basement, and every year, the latkes were the same: flat and gray and cold and bland. Not that she didn't like latkes. She'd had some amazing latkes at Grandma Trudy's house, but they were a

completely different food than the slippery circles
of felt they served at temple. Too bad they couldn't
serve piña colada fritters instead.

Or mozzarella cheese fritters.

Or chocolate-marshmallow fritters.

Penina dropped her fork. "Zozo!" she said.
"There's practically no difference between a fritter
and a latke. You could make a latke out of anything
you want—as long as you fry it. The potato isn't the
important part. It's the oil!"

"Mmm," agreed Zozo. Her mouth was full.

Penina stood up and paced the kitchen. "This is
huge. This changes everything!"

8. Everything in the Whole Entire World Goes Wrong

The green olive latkes were the worst. Everyone agreed on that, but they all had different ideas about which ones were the best.

"I like the pinto bean and salsa ones," said Dad.

"They're good, but I prefer the pumpkin latkes with nutmeg," said Mom.

"My favorite latkes are the peanut butter and jelly!" Mimsy announced.

Zozo didn't vote. She'd had to leave before the Levine Family Latke Fest was finished, but Penina thought they would both have picked the piña coladas. The first batch had been the best. Lots of others were good, though. After they'd decided to make more batches, Zozo had run next door for extra ingredients. She brought back canned corn, frozen blueberries, and a special allergen-free baking mix, since they needed something floury for the latkes, and Zozo was allergic to wheat.

"This was nice, Penina," said Mom. "Anytime you want to make dinner, be my guest."

"It's my turn to pick the candles!" yelled Mimsy.

Penina smushed her fork into the green olive latke she'd pushed to the side of her plate. It was a brown blob with green rings showing through. It looked diseased.

Mom jumped up. "Okay, Mimsy. What colors do you want?"

"Purple! No, pink! No, yellow! No, purple *and* yellow! No, purple and pink!" Mimsy and Mom walked into the living room together, with Mimsy choosing colors at the top of her lungs.

There were still a couple of latkes left. Penina put a pumpkin one on her plate.

Dad stood up and pushed in his chair. "Come on, Pen. Let's say the blessing. Then you can pick out another gift to open."

Penina used her fork to break off a piece of pumpkin latke. "I'm not done yet," she said. Hadn't they been in the middle of dinner? A dinner *Penina* had made?

"It's getting dark," said Dad, "time to light the menorah."

So? It wasn't dark yet. They could have put off lighting the menorah for five more minutes. If it had been *Penina's* turn to pick the candles and *Mimsy's* special homemade dinner, they would have waited.

"Two pink, one purple, and a yellow *shamash!*" Mimsy yelled from the next room. "Hurry up! We're lighting them!"

Penina took a bite of latke. She'd go light the candles when she was good and ready.

"Penina," said Dad, "let's make this a nice Hanukkah, okay? Don't be like this."

Like what? Like wanting to finish her latke before Mimsy took over the whole entire holiday? Penina chewed slowly.

The kitchen door swung open, and Mom leaned in. "Ready? We're lighting the menorah."

"I'm not," said Penina.

"Excuse me?" said Mom. "Is this the same Penina Levine who delivered the lecture about the true meaning of Hanukkah? The very same Miss Levine who advocates the abandonment of the gift-giving tradition that we might better contemplate the miracle of the oil?"

"Yeah, well, latkes symbolize the miracle of the oil, too, you know!" Penina shouted.

"Of course they do," said Mom. She stood in the

53

kitchen doorway with her arms crossed. "We ate the latkes. They were very good, but now it's time to light the menorah. It's your sister's turn to pick the candles. Last night was your turn. Tomorrow will be your turn again." She spoke slowly and clearly, as if Penina were a preschooler, or just a very, very stupid sixth grader.

"It's not that!" Penina said. Oh, great. Now she was starting to cry. She clamped her jaw shut to keep the crying in, but it didn't work. Her nose was clogged, so she had to breathe through her mouth, and when she unclenched her jaw to take a breath, a big, wet sob came out of it.

Mom uncrossed her arms and held her hands up, palms out. "Whoa, whoa," she uttered.

"I'm not a horse!" Penina shouted. Why was Mom *whoa*ing her? Couldn't she just listen for once in her life?

"I know you're not," said Mom. She put her hand on Penina's shoulder. Penina jerked away. She didn't want a pat or a cuddle. She just wanted—

Penina blew her nose in a napkin. She took another one and wiped her eyes. She stood up and took a step toward the doorway. "Okay, fine," she said. "Let's get it over with."

"Well, that's not a very festive attitude," Dad said.

Penina didn't bother to answer. She thought she saw Mom give Dad a signal to "hush," but she wasn't sure. Mom lit the candles, and they all sang the blessing. Penina sang very softly, but she did sing. It wasn't the menorah's fault that everything in the whole entire world was going wrong.

"I hope you don't have a lot of homework, Pen," said Dad, "It's getting late."

Oh, yeah. Homework.

Penina found her backpack and got out her take-home folder. It wasn't too bad. She had a Social Studies worksheet and a chapter to read for Language Arts, but that was it. Except for the note.

It was on textured stationery the color of French vanilla ice cream—pretty paper for an ugly note. It started "Dear Parent," and ended, "Sincerely, Thomas Tobin, Ed.D.," and it pretty much summed up what Dr. Tobin had told them in school that day.

Penina took it by one corner and dropped it on her mother's lap.

"Oh, poor Mrs. Brown," said Mom.

Poor Mrs. Brown? How about poor Penina?

9. A Pink-and-Yellow Bikini

"Fa la la la la, la la la la," sang Zozo.

"Troll the ancient yuletide carol," sang Penina.

"That's not how it goes," said Zozo. She stopped where she was, and the lady who'd been walking behind them almost plowed her massive stroller right into Zozo.

Penina leaped aside. The lady swerved around Zozo and kept right on going.

"What's her hurry?" said Zozo.

"She's probably trying to find her kid," Penina said.

"Why?"

"Did you see her stroller? It was loaded with packages. The thing was full of boxes and bags, but I didn't see any kid in it."

Zozo shrugged. "Maybe she's letting him wait in line to see Santa while she goes shopping."

They leaned over the railing to look down on

the lower level of the mall. They could see Santa on his throne and a long line of kids and parents and strollers and shopping bags spiraling around the North Pole setup. Penina looked at the line, trying to tell which kid might belong to the stroller lady. "Fa la la la la, la la la la," she sang softly. She could *not* get that song out of her head.

"It's *trill* the ancient yuletide carol, not *troll*," said Zozo.

"It's troll," Penina said. It was. Her mom had a book, *Ten-Thousand Traditional Songs for Piano and Guitar*, and it had that song in it. And it said *troll*. Penina remembered, because she'd seen it and thought that it was weird. Trolls lived under bridges and ate goats. They didn't have anything to do with Christmas.

"*Troll* doesn't even make sense," said Zozo. "How can it be *troll*?"

"It just is," said Penina. It didn't make sense, but it was catchy. The song was embedded in her brain. The more Penina tried not to sing it, the more it crowded out every other thought in her head. La la la la.

"Penina, I sang it in choir. I think I know the words," Zozo said.

"Well, you know the wrong words, then," said Penina.

Zozo gave Penina a *look*. Then she turned quickly, so her long, shiny black ponytail swung out dramatically. She took a step away from Penina and looked back over her shoulder. "Come on, let's go in here."

She strode across the hall into a fancy clothing shop. Penina scrambled after her. She held her big shopping bag ahead of her to push through the crowds. There was nothing fragile in it, just Mimsy's stuffed cat. Penina had finally gotten it. Now she just needed something for Zozo. And maybe Mrs. Brown.

Penina had been to the mall a zillion times, but she had never been inside this store. It was crowded in there. Not that there were so many customers—Zozo and Penina were practically the only ones there—but the place was packed with racks and racks of clothing. Penina followed Zozo, and they wedged themselves between a display of sparkly party dresses and a row of multicolored swimming suits. Zozo pulled out a pink-and-yellow bikini.

"May I help you?" asked the saleslady. She looked a little like an older Zozo, if Zozo were blond and blue-eyed and cheerful and friendly.

"No, thanks, just looking," said Zozo.

It was twenty degrees and snowing outside. Why did Zozo want to look at swimming suits?

"Are you going on vacation someplace sunny?" asked the saleslady.

Penina ran her hand along the swimming suit display. One of the suits came with a flowy greeny-blue wrap. Penina let the fabric slide between her fingers. It was slippery, like something a mermaid would wear.

"Yeah," said Zozo, "my mom and I are going to Aruba."

Penina dropped the wrap and stared at Zozo. Zozo was staring at the pink-and-yellow bikini, but she turned to face Penina. "I was going to tell you," Zozo said. She gave Penina a half-embarrassed smile. "But, well . . ."

"Okay, you girls look through the suits," said the saleslady. "Let me know if you find anything you want to try on." She took off and disappeared into the maze of clothing racks.

Penina tried to remember where Aruba was. Someplace tropical, someplace with sunshine and palm trees and warm, sandy beaches strewn with beautiful, exotic shells. "Oh, that's great! Have a good time!" she said to Zozo.

"We're staying at this hotel that's right on the beach, and you get free snorkeling lessons. My mom says I can go snorkeling. I might get to swim with dolphins."

"Oh, that's great! Have a good time!" said Penina. She knew she'd already said it, but she didn't have anything else to say. She couldn't say, for instance, "How come you get to go on a fabulous tropical vacation and I have to stay here in the frozen slush?"

Zozo pulled a black bikini off the rack and held it with the pink-and-yellow one. "My mom says I should get two—one to wear while the other dries, since we'll be swimming every day."

"That's great! That sounds great!" said Penina. Her mouth had taken over the conversation, since her brain wanted nothing to do with it.

"We're leaving after school on Friday. It's a really long trip, but then we'll get to spend Christmas on the beach!" Zozo said.

"When are you coming back?" Penina asked.

"The thirtieth, the day before New Year's Eve.

Hey! Do you want to do something for New Year's? Maybe a sleepover? I'll invite Jackie and Anne, and I'll show you all my Aruba pictures!"

"That's great! That sounds great!" said Penina. Back to that again. A week. Zozo was going to be gone for a week. She wasn't coming back till almost the last day of vacation. She'd miss everything—presents and sled riding and hot chocolate—and if Penina wanted to do anything, she'd have to do it all by herself. Anne would be babysitting every day of vacation, and Jackie lived way out in the country. Penina couldn't count on seeing them. She would be alone. Except for Mimsy.

"All right!" Zozo said. "I'll tell my mom to get us that bubbly grape juice so we can toast the New Year, and we'll get all dressed up. Hey, maybe I'll get something to wear in Aruba. I bet they have beautiful clothes there!"

"Uh-huh," Penina said.

"Penina! Don't worry. I'll bring something back for you," Zozo said.

Penina didn't want clothes from Aruba. She wanted her friend with her over vacation. She wanted Mrs. Brown to change her mind and stay in Marionville. She wanted to get out of that store. It was cramped in there, with so many overflowing clothes racks, and the music was too loud. *Fa la la la la, la la la la.*

"You don't need to get me anything," Penina said. She didn't want anything from Aruba. Besides, by the time Zozo got back, Hanukkah and Christmas would both be over.

"I'll get you something really good," promised Zozo. "I know! I'll bring back all those little soaps they give you for free at the hotel."

Penina didn't know what to say. She didn't want to say "Great!" again, so she just smiled at Zozo. Or tried to.

"Kidding!" Zozo said. "I'll bring you back a coral bracelet. They have really nice coral in Aruba. We could have matching friendship bracelets."

Wasn't coral made from an endangered species of sea life? Wouldn't wearing a coral bracelet be like announcing to the world you don't care about animals? Penina hoped Zozo wouldn't bring her a bracelet like that. She could never wear it.

10. Ablaze

The stuffed cat was too soft and lumpy to wrap in paper, so Penina stuck it in a big pink-checkered gift bag, with the Sunday comics arranged inside to hide the cat. She added it to Mimsy's pile of gifts. It was the largest one there.

"Here you go, girls," said Mom. "Open these." She handed Penina a neatly wrapped present. It was about the size of a shoe box but much heavier than any pair of shoes Penina had ever worn.

"Shouldn't we light the candles first?" said Penina. The lines at the mall had been forever, and then Mrs. Miller had to stop for gas on the way home, and by the time Penina got back from the mall, it was already dark. They really should light the menorah before doing anything else. Besides, it was Penina's turn to pick the candles. She was going to pick all blues, to match her mood. Too bad they didn't have *black* Hanukkah candles.

"No, no," said Mom. "We want you to have these first."

"Oh, goody!" Mimsy yelled. She was already destroying the wrapping on her present.

Penina sat down on the couch with her heavy present. It had a real cloth ribbon. Penina's family always used curling ribbon or stick-on bows. This gift must have been wrapped in the store.

"Oh! Thank you! Just what I always wanted!" Mimsy shouted. She ran and bounced and twirled so much that Penina couldn't even tell what she'd gotten. But Mimsy stopped long enough to hold her gift out in front of her and announce, "My very own menorah!"

It looked like the big menorah, but in miniature: brass, with eight curved branches with places for the candles, and a ninth place in the middle for the *shamash*. Penina shook her box. It sounded like the exact same thing. She opened her box. It was.

"Thanks," Penina said.

Mom and Dad were grinning their heads off. "We figured it was time," said Dad.

"Now you won't have to fight about whose turn it is to pick the candles," said Mom.

If a backhanded compliment was a compliment that was really an insult, then this so-called gift was a backhanded present. She was surprised Mom and Dad hadn't engraved it with the words "Since you never learned to share nicely."

"And I got extra candles, too, so there will be plenty to go around," Mom said. She handed a box of candles to Mimsy and dropped a box on Penina's lap. "Come on, girls. Let's light the menorah. I mean, the *menorahs*."

It was the fourth night. They'd need four candles plus the *shamash*. Penina found five blue candles and put them in her brand-new menorah.

Mimsy had all different colors, with a long explanation about each one. "Pink is my favorite color, and purple is my second favorite color, and blue is sort of like purple, but it's not my third favorite color. My third favorite color is yellow, but I do like blue, but not as much as yellow, so the *shamash* is yellow . . ."

Penina wondered if Mimsy would say the blessing or just keep right on talking about her candles while everybody else sang.

While Mimsy told them all about her candle choices, Mom and Dad put candles in the big menorah, all white. It looked elegant.

Mom lit her *shamash* and used it to light the *shamash* on Penina's menorah, then Mimsy's. Penina

sang the blessing and lit her very own menorah. It wasn't as impressive as the big menorah, but it was pretty.

The Temple menorah had been six feet high, made of pure gold.

Now *that* was an impressive menorah. Mrs. Greenbaum had told them that when the Maccabees rededicated the Temple, the big gold menorah was gone. The Maccabees made their own menorah out of spears. It wasn't as glamorous as the fancy gold menorah, but it did the job. Penina imagined the miraculous light in the rededicated Temple. It must have reflected off the stone and the sand all around. It must have been beautiful.

The mountain of presents had been sparkly even when it was reflecting the light of just one menorah. Now that it was in the room with three menorahs, it was practically ablaze.

11. Arrested or Fired?

"She got arrested. My neighbor's cousin saw it on the news. She took, like, a million dollars from the school's bank account."

"Nuh-uh. She got fired, but it wasn't for taking money. Dr. Tobin found out she'd been posting really mean things about him on her blog."

"She did *not* get fired. She quit. She got a job with the CIA, but it's top secret, so she can't talk about it."

Penina hung up her coat, took off her boots, and listened to the rumors fly up and down the hallway. Everyone had an opinion about why Mrs. Brown was leaving, but Penina didn't believe any of them. If Mrs. Brown had gotten arrested or fired or gotten a new job, then why would she be coming back today and tomorrow?

Even Zozo had a version of the Mrs. Brown story. "She's in this animal rights group where they're always rescuing animals from labs and slaughterhouses, and they're planning this big raid on a fur-coat factory, so she had to quit teaching to get ready for that."

"Zozo!" Penina said. "That's not true."

"It is so. Didn't you ever see the bumper stickers on her car?"

"So? That doesn't mean anything." Penina sometimes saw Mrs. Brown in the teachers' parking lot, getting into a small tan car. It had two stickers on the rear bumper. One said "Be kind to animals: Don't eat them." The other said, "Live simply, that others might simply live." But that wasn't the same thing as being an animal-rights outlaw.

Zozo lined up her boots in her locker and stepped into her shiny school shoes. "Well, how do you explain it, then?"

Penina couldn't just step into her shoes. She had to unbuckle them, pull up her saggy socks, shove her feet into her scuffy shoes, and then buckle them. She leaned against her open locker with her left foot balanced on her right thigh. She struggled with the buckle as she answered Zozo. "The same way Dr. Tobin did. She has a family emergency."

Zozo closed her locker and leaned against it with her arms crossed. "Don't you get it?" she said. "'Family emergency' is just something they say when they don't want you to know the real reason. Like, when no one could print anything in the computer lab because no one knew how to set up the new printer, and they said it was due to 'technical difficulties'?"

Penina remembered.

"Well," Zozo explained, "'family emergency' is like 'technical difficulties.' It's just what they say, not what they mean."

"Come on, it probably was a family emergency." Hadn't Mrs. Brown been crying on Monday? Besides, what else except for a true family emergency could make Mrs. Brown just leave? Just quit in the middle of the school year? Just abandon them without even telling them why? Penina finished putting on her shoes and gave her locker door a good, hard slam. "And anyway," Penina added, "It's not even definite she's going. We can probably still get her to stay. We have to explain to her that we need her here. She's the best teacher we ever had."

Zozo didn't answer, just pressed her lips together.

"What?"

No answer from Zozo, just pressed lips and wide-open eyes, staring past Penina.

Penina turned around.

"I didn't mean to eavesdrop," said Mrs. Brown.

Penina had no idea how long the teacher had been there. She'd been behind Penina's open locker door.

"But I'm kind of glad I did." Mrs. Brown gave another one of those sad-clown smiles. "I know people are curious about the reasons for my sudden leave of absence. After homeroom, I'll do my best to explain."

The homeroom bell rang, and Mrs. Brown turned and walked into the classroom. Penina and Zozo followed her. There didn't seem to be anything else to do.

"Do you think she heard us?" Penina whispered to Zozo, once they were at their desks.

"Gee, I don't know. You *think*?" Zozo answered.

Penina didn't blame her. If *Penina* had been the one saying Mrs. Brown was committing crimes while *Zozo* was calling her the best teacher on the planet, Penina would have been angry, too.

They had to say the Pledge of Allegiance and sing the national anthem and listen to the morning announcements. That would give Zozo plenty of time to cool down.

After the announcements, it was time for Social Studies, but Mrs. Brown didn't tell them to get out their textbooks. Instead, she stood in the front of the room and said, "I'd like to thank you. Mrs. Fisk told me you were model students this week."

Mrs. Fisk had been their sub. She was okay, but not very energetic. She had sort of slumped around

73

the classroom for two days, yawning. Penina hoped Mrs. Fisk wasn't the one who was going to take Mrs. Brown's place permanently. Not that anyone would, of course, because Mrs. Brown wasn't really going to leave.

Penina thought about chaining herself to the teacher's desk until Mrs. Brown promised to stay after all. She'd read a book about a girl doing that. Penina thought the book was called *Keep Ms. Sugarman in the Fourth Grade*. She wasn't sure. It had been a while since she'd read it. If Penina *did* chain herself to Mrs. Brown's desk, how long would she have to stay there? What if she had to go to the bathroom? She didn't remember how the girl in the book had handled that.

"As you know," said Mrs. Brown, "tomorrow will be my last day teaching in this school. Dr. Tobin discussed this with you on Tuesday, but I thought you might have questions for me. I'd like to take a few minutes and answer them now."

Dead silence in the classroom. The minute hand on the clock moved ahead with a loud *click*, then everything was quiet again. Penina bit her pencil, just to have something to hear.

"I want to be honest with you," Mrs. Brown said, "but I don't want to burden you with a lot of unnecessary information. So let me just ask you again: Any questions?"

No questions, but there was a round of throat clearing. Also some squeaking chairs and a pencil falling on the floor.

"Okay, well, if I were a sixth grader, and if my teacher were taking an unexpected leave of absence, I would probably want to know where she was going, and why," said Mrs. Brown.

Penina nodded. Everyone did. Zozo's ponytails swayed and made her nod look like she really meant it. Zozo had two ponytails today, one behind each ear. Yesterday, at the mall, she'd had one ponytail in the back. Penina knew Zozo was working out a system—a hairdo for every day of the week. Monday was braid day, one big braid in the back. Tuesday was two braids, one on each side. Tomorrow was Friday, and Zozo would probably wear what she called a "quarter up," part of her hair in a little ponytail with the rest loose. Penina sometimes tried to match Zozo's hairdos, but not on Fridays. Penina couldn't let part of her hair be loose. If she tried that, it poofed out and puffed around her head in a crazy, frizzy mess. She kept her hair in braids or ponytails. Always.

"So let me just tell you what I'd want to know, if

I were in your shoes," said Mrs. Brown. Her hair wasn't crazy or frizzy or sway-y or glossy. It was smooth, grayish brown, a little wavy. She had quiet hair. "My sister is very ill. She lives in Arizona, so I will be moving there to take care of her."

Penina crunched her teeth into her pencil. Mrs. Brown wasn't going to change her mind. If her sick sister was in Arizona, she couldn't stay here. She had to go to Arizona. That was far. That was completely different from Marionville, Pennsylvania. Did they even have trees in Arizona? Did they even have water? Or was it all cactuses and weird rock formations?

"Are you coming back, once your sister gets

better?" asked Suzie. Penina was glad someone had asked. If Suzie hadn't done it, Penina would have had to.

"Well, that's hard to say," said Mrs. Brown. "They don't—I mean—we don't—that is, well—it's hard to predict."

It was obvious they weren't getting the whole story here, but Penina didn't think Mrs. Brown was trying to avoid answering them. It was more like she was trying to avoid answering *herself*. She didn't like it any more than Penina did, but there was nothing anybody could do about it.

Mrs. Brown was leaving. She was never coming back.

12. "Choose Your Weapon"

"Hold on a minute," Zozo commanded. She dropped her backpack at Penina's feet and went charging up a pile of snow plowed against the side of the car dealership they passed on their way home.

If only Zozo would hurry. The longer Penina stood around waiting for Zozo, the more melting snow seeped through her mittens, her boots, her hat and hood and scarf.

Zozo stood at the summit of her snow mound and broke off two giant icicles from the "Great Deals!" sign above her. She ran-and-slid back down and pointed one of them at Penina. *"En garde!"* she shouted.

"Not fair, I'm unarmed," Penina answered.

Zozo pointed both icicles toward the ground and held them out to Penina. "Choose your weapon," she said.

They looked alike, but maybe the one on the right was a little pointier. Penina took it.

They had a duel there on the slushy sidewalk. It didn't last long. They could only clash a few times before the icicles broke all to pieces. Penina thought about licking her icicle end, but it was probably

filthy. She dropped it on a snow drift as they walked past. It made a hole in the top layer of snow.

"That's my favorite part of winter," said Zozo. "Icicle sword fights."

"Yeah," Penina said. She liked them, too. They hadn't had many this year. It wasn't easy to find the right kind of icicle.

"What's your favorite?" Zozo asked.

Penina didn't know. Slush in her boots? Frozen ears? Teachers leaving? Friends taking off for tropical islands? "How about my *least* favorite thing?"

Zozo made an impatient sound with her teeth. "*Tsk!* What is *with* you?"

Penina made the sound back. "*Tsk!* What do you mean?"

"It's been Whiny Wednesday with you all week."

Penina had to smile at that. It was an old joke. Their school used to have Motivation Days: Marvelous Mondays, Terrific Tuesdays, Winning Wednesdays, Thankful Thursdays, Friendship Fridays. Dr. Tobin would get on the announcements and remind them to be marvelous or friendly or whatever day it was. Penina and Zozo had made up alternate days: Macho Monday (for spitting and swaggering), Torpid Tuesday (for sitting around doing nothing). Whiny Wednesday was for whining —complaining about everything, sulking. (*Kvetching,* as her grandmother would say. For some things, Yiddish was better.)

The Motivation Days had kind of phased out. Their alternate days did, too, after a while. Penina hadn't thought about them in a long time.

"So what?" Penina said. "If you weren't about to escape to paradise, you'd be whiny, too."

"See, that's just what I mean. I can't help it if I'm going to Aruba. Why do you have to be so whiny about it?"

Of course Zozo could help it. If she wanted to, she could just tell her mother she didn't want to go. She could tell her she'd rather stay and hang out with Penina, her best friend, her friend who meant more to her than all the dolphin rides and coral bracelets in the universe.

If Penina had the chance to swim with dolphins, *she* would give it up if Zozo needed company over winter vacation. Penina was about 90 percent sure she would. Well, maybe 80 percent sure. Well, no, probably not. If Penina had the chance to race through the waves, laughing and squeaking in perfect harmony with her adopted dolphin pod, she'd take it. And the thing was, Zozo would *want* her to take it. She'd be happy for her. That was the difference between Penina and Zozo.

"I know. I'm sorry," Penina said. "Mimsy's been

81

driving me crazy. I don't know how I'm going to survive winter vacation. With you in Aruba, it's going to be all Mimsy, all the time."

"Oh, yeah," said Zozo. "I hadn't thought of that." They splashed through a few more slush puddles. Then Zozo added, "Well, at least your grandparents are coming. That will be fun, won't it?"

Penina shrugged. She loved Grandma and Grandpa. She couldn't wait to see them, but they weren't the kind of grandparents who played outside in the snow. They were the kind of grandparents who played board games. *Bored* games. And they would probably want to include Mimsy.

"What do you think is wrong with Mrs. Brown's sister?" Penina asked. Dropping everything and moving to Arizona, that was pretty much the ultimate good-sister challenge.

"Don't know. Cancer, probably. When someone says 'very sick,' they usually mean cancer."

"Is that how it was with your dad?" As soon as Penina asked, she felt like the wind was cutting right through her winter coat. She shuddered. This was *not* a good topic of conversation. This was *not* something she and Zozo talked about. She should never have brought it up.

"Nah, that was his heart. I just mean generally.

People don't talk about cancer. They call it the 'big C.'"

The big C. The big see. The big sea.

"Do you think Mrs. Brown is the big sister or the little sister?" Penina asked. She'd never thought about that before. Before today, she hadn't really thought about Mrs. Brown having a family at all.

"Well, since Mrs. Brown is about fifty years old, I'm guessing neither one of them is the little sister," Zozo said.

"You know what I mean. Is Mrs. Brown older or younger?" Because Penina could not imagine transplanting herself to the desert or someplace to look after Mimsy, if Mimsy got sick. And she sure couldn't imagine Mimsy coming to take care of her. Unless there were some kind of prize involved or lots of admirers to impress somehow by doing it. "Maybe they're twins. Twins are supposed to have a special bond, aren't they?"

Zozo cackled. "Uh, Penina, aren't *sisters* supposed to have a special bond, whether they're twins or not?"

Zozo was an only child. She had no idea what she was talking about. "Well," said Penina, "they don't have to."

Zozo stopped to pick red berries off a yew hedge. Penina stopped, too. She loved those things. It was hard to hold them without squishing them, but they were so pretty—scarlet and smooth and startling against the dark green bush in the bright white snow.

She picked a round, fat one and held it up in the sunlight. "This is it," Penina said. "This is my favorite thing about winter. Picking the red yew berries."

"Yeah, mine, too," said Zozo.

"Not icicle sword fights?"

"Well, tied," Zozo admitted.

"Yeah, and tied with sledding, too," said Penina.

"And with building snow forts," Zozo added.

"And catching snowflakes on your tongue!" Penina shouted. She felt a little less whiny, for the first time in days. She was still sad, though. She felt bad for Mrs. Brown. Arizona probably didn't have yew berries or sled riding or icicles.

But it would have snowflakes.

"Hey, Zozo, can you come over after supper?" *If you're not too busy packing suntan lotion and flip-flops, that is?*

"Sure, why?"

"We're going to make a good-bye present for Mrs. Brown."

13. A Zillion Zillion Snowflakes

Fifth night.

Six candles.

Three menorahs.

Eighteen lights.

"Wow. That looks so—fiery," said Zozo. "I feel like we should roast marshmallows over it or something."

Penina was pretty sure they shouldn't. It was probably against Jewish law, and it was definitely against Levine family law. She knew what Zozo meant, though. As they added menorahs and candles and lights, it was beginning to look like they had a bonfire going in their living room window.

They went up to Penina's room. Zozo upended her tote bag over Penina's bedspread and spilled out a collection of supplies—hole punches, glitter glue, craft scissors, nail scissors, scissors with wavy blades for cutting scalloped edges. "Are we thinking more

85

like snowstorm, or more like blizzard?" Zozo asked.

Penina tossed her supplies onto the bed—a compass, jar lids for tracing, pencils, more glitter glue, and a ream of paper. It was thin white printer paper, only it jammed the printer, so they never used it in the machine. Her dad had said she could have it; no one used onionskin paper anymore anyway.

"I'm thinking blizzard," Penina said, "a massive, school-closing, road-blocking, power-line-downing blizzard."

"Yeah, me, too," said Zozo. "We better work fast."

But you couldn't rush snowflake making, Penina found out. If she just made a few quick cuts in her snowflake, it turned out pretty ordinary looking. But if she really got into it, cutting unusual shapes with the craft scissors, using the nail scissors to make teeny snips, she wound up with lacy, filigreed paper snowflakes that were so delicate they could hardly open up without tearing. They were exquisite, and no two were alike.

Penina and Zozo cut a zillion zillion snowflakes. They rolled on glitter glue and spread them around Penina's room to dry.

"Oh my goodness! Are you still here?" exclaimed Mom. She opened Penina's door the rest of the way

and stepped into the room, avoiding a drift of paper snowflakes beside the bookcase.

"Mrs. Miller said it was okay," Penina answered.

"I'm sorry, Mrs. Levine," Zozo said at the same time. "I was just leaving."

"That's okay, Zozo," said Mom. "I don't mean to kick you out. It's just . . ." Mom looked like she wanted to sit down, but the bed, the desk chair, and the floor were all covered in snowflakes. "You know, it's ten thirty at night. I thought you went home hours ago. It's been so quiet up here, I thought Penina had fallen asleep."

"We're making a good-bye present for Mrs. Brown," Penina said.

"But we're just about finished. I have to go anyway," said Zozo. She got up and started throwing things into her bag—craft scissors, hole punch, some of Penina's pencils.

"Oh, sorry," said Zozo. She put back the pencils.

Penina and her mother walked Zozo to the door and stood on the porch to watch her walk home. They saw Zozo's porch light flash twice to signal that she was inside, safe and sound.

"You better get ready for bed, Penina," said Mom. "Big day tomorrow. When you get home from school, Grandma and Grandpa will be here."

And Mrs. Brown would be gone.

14. Too Rushed, Too Public, Too Messy

Penina didn't know what she'd been expecting, maybe a big teary scene, with all the class gathering around Mrs. Brown for a group hug. Maybe a ceremony to honor Mrs. Brown's years of teaching with a certificate or cake or something. Maybe a last-minute change of plans—Mrs. Brown's sister gets better and Mrs. Brown doesn't have to leave after all.

But it wasn't anything like that. It was just like any other school day, except that it was the day before winter vacation, and they didn't have regular classes. They had intramural sports or library period. They had time to clean out their lockers. They had a DVD of *Bridge to Terabithia*, and they had two minutes before the dismissal bell to copy down a few lines of information Mrs. Brown had written on the board. "This will be my address in Arizona.

I hope you will all keep in touch," she said.

Penina copied the address onto her take-home folder. Tucson, Arizona. It made Penina think of cowboys and cactuses and coyotes. She'd never been out west, but she had the idea that everything out there was orangey-yellow. And hot. And dry.

The dismissal bell rang, and everyone tore out into the hallway, everyone except Penina and Zozo. Penina was going over the address she'd written in her folder, checking it against the one on the board. She wanted to make sure she'd gotten it exactly right. Zozo was waiting by Penina's desk.

"Okay, we better do it now," said Zozo. She'd convinced Penina that they shouldn't give Mrs. Brown the present first thing in the morning, because it would have been too rushed, and they shouldn't do it during school because it would have been too public, and they shouldn't do it during lunch because it would have been too messy. So they'd decided to wait till after school.

Penina had the present ready. She'd put all the snowflakes into a big gift box. She'd used her best gel pen to write on it.

To: Mrs. Brown.

Good Luck. We'll miss you!

From: Penina and Zozo.

Penina and Zozo went up to the teacher's desk. Penina handed the box to the teacher.

"What's this?" said Mrs. Brown.

"It's a going-away present," said Zozo.

"Well, thank you," said Mrs. Brown. "Shall I open it now?" She already had her fingers under the lid. Zozo and Penina nodded.

Mrs. Brown opened the box and pulled out a handful of paper snowflakes, and another and another. They drifted across her desk and wafted down to the floor, their silver glitter glue glimmering and shimmering. "Oh, thank you," said Mrs. Brown. "They're lovely!"

"We made them for you," said Zozo.

"We thought that you would miss the snow," Penina added.

"I will miss it," Mrs. Brown said, "but not as much as I will miss you. You've been a fantastic class this year. You made me love coming to work every day."

That Mrs. Brown sure was a crier. It made Penina feel a little better, because Penina was a crier, too. Penina and Mrs. Brown stood there with their red eyes and dripping noses, sniffling and snuffling, while Zozo observed them placidly.

"We're sorry about your sister, Mrs. Brown. We hope she'll be okay," Zozo said.

"And we're sorry you have to leave," said Penina.
"We really wish you could stay here."

"Thank you," said Mrs. Brown. She wiped her
eyes with a wrinkly tissue from her pocket. "I hate to
leave, too, but, you know, you are going to be just
fine. You're good students and strong learners. You're
going to knock your new teacher's socks off!"

Mrs. Brown looked like she was trying to smile.

Penina tried, too, but she just made a little twitch of her mouth. It would have been a smile, but she didn't have the energy to keep it up.

"We'll write to you," Penina pledged.

"I'll look forward to your letters," said Mrs. Brown. She fluffed up the pile of snowflakes. "And I'll hang these up in my kitchen. They'll look just perfect in the window above the sink."

"Have you already seen your new house?" asked Zozo.

Mrs. Brown smiled, a real smile this time, but a small one. "It's my old house, the house I grew up in. My sister lives there now, and I know she'll appreciate the snowflakes as much as I do."

"Is she your little sister or your big sister?" Penina asked. That sounded so babyish. She wished she'd said "older or younger" instead. Actually, she wished she'd said something completely different, or—better yet—nothing at all.

"She's my big sister, my much bigger sister. She was thirteen when I was born."

"Do you have her picture?" asked Zozo. Penina wished she'd thought to ask that.

Mrs. Brown did, in her wallet. She took it out and showed them a thin woman with thin hair and a thin smile, nothing like Mrs. Brown.

"She's very pretty," Zozo said.

"Please tell her we hope she's feeling better," Penina said.

"I will," said Mrs. Brown. "Thank you, girls. This was very thoughtful."

You didn't hug teachers. Penina didn't know if it was an actual school rule or just common sense, but she knew it wouldn't be right to put her arms around Mrs. Brown and press her face into her woolly chocolate-colored sweater.

Mrs. Brown put out her hand, and Penina shook it. Mrs. Brown put her other hand on top of Penina's and gave it a couple of gentle pats. She did the same with Zozo.

"Have a good vacation, girls," Mrs. Brown said.

"You, too," said Penina, even though Mrs. Brown wasn't going on vacation.

And that was it. That was the last thing Penina said to Mrs. Brown. The last thing she would ever say to her, unless she called her on the phone someday, which she couldn't imagine doing.

Penina and Zozo walked home slowly, so slowly they were almost walking home in the dark. The days were short now. It was a good time of year for menorahs and colored lights and Yule logs, anything to cut through the darkness.

They didn't stop to pick yew berries or have icicle fights, but at the top of their street, about a block from home, Zozo froze in her tracks. She put her hand on Penina's arm, and Penina stopped, too. "Wow," Zozo said.

Penina tried to look where Zozo was looking, but Zozo was gazing all around them. It had started to snow while they were walking, and now everything was covered in sparkling white. No footprints, no tire marks, no slush, just a fresh, endless blanket of snow.

"It's beautiful," said Penina, "like we're inside a snow globe."

"It's terrible," said Zozo. "Now I'll never make it to the airport."

15. Grandma's Revenge

"Penina, darling! You're home! We were just about to harness the dogs to the sled and go out looking for you!" Grandma grabbed Penina in a big hug, kissed her, and passed her to Grandpa.

He hugged her, but he let go fast. "Penina, you're covered with snow!"

"Of course she's covered with snow. It's snowing out!" said Grandma. She took Penina's coat and hung it up in the hall closet. She took her hat, gloves, and scarf and shouted into the living room, "Sonia, put these in the dryer, and put some hot cocoa on for the girls. Penina is soaked to the skin."

It was nice and warm in the house. Penina felt her face thawing where Grandma and Grandpa had kissed it, but her fingers were still mostly frozen. Grandma put her hand over Penina's frozen fingers. "Oh, my! You're hand is like ice! Come in and get warm. Sonia, Penina's home!"

Mom hustled in from the kitchen, wiping her hands on her blue-and-white frilly apron. Penina didn't think she had ever seen her mother in an apron before. It looked weird, like she was missing a high, puffy chef's hat. "Hi, honey," said Mom. "Where were you? We were worried. Did you say hi to Grandma and Grandpa?"

"Of course she said hi to us," answered Grandma. "You think she wouldn't say hi to her grandparents who traveled all the way from Peekskill just to see her?"

"Pina!" yelled Mimsy. She zoomed in circles around Penina, Mom, Grandma, and Grandpa. Once she slowed down, Penina could tell she was wearing a blue-and-white frilly apron, just like Mom's—but smaller. "Grandma and Grandpa are here! They said I could open one present, even though you weren't here yet, and I opened one, and it was really two presents because it had a present inside the pocket, so I got this apron and Hanukkah *gelt*, and Mommy has an apron just like it because Grandma made them for both of us and now Mommy and I match so I can help her make the latkes!"

"Don't worry, Penina," Grandma said. She hadn't ever let go of Penina's hand. "There's an apron for you, too."

Penina wasn't worried. She didn't care if Mimsy

and Mom had matching aprons. Penina and Zozo had already made twenty-seven varieties of latke—without any kind of apron whatsoever.

"Go tell your dad you're home, Penina. He was concerned about you," Mom said.

"Let her have some hot cocoa first, Sonia," Grandma said. She was really crushing Penina's hand. Penina hadn't known her grandmother was so strong. "She just walked home through a blizzard."

"I'll tell him," Grandpa volunteered. "He'll be glad to know you're home, kiddle." Grandpa gave Penina a nice thump on the back and took off. "You coming, Mimsy?" he called over his shoulder.

"Let me tell him!" yelled Mimsy. She chased Grandpa down to the den. "I saw Penina come in, so I can tell Daddy she's home, and . . ." Penina quit listening. She concentrated on getting her hand back from Grandma.

"Penina likes walking home from school. It's good exercise," said Mom, "and she talks and laughs the whole time with her friend Zozo, don't you, Penina?"

What was the question? Was Mom asking if Penina liked walking or if she talked and laughed the whole time with Zozo?

Neither one. Mom wasn't asking anything. She was still talking. "That's probably what took her so long, not just the snow. She and Zozo were probably chattering up a storm, weren't you, Penina?"

Was this an actual question this time? "Well,"
Penina said, "I'm—"

"Regardless," Grandma cut her off. "The child is
freezing, and unless she gets something hot to drink,
she's going to get double pneumonia." She let go of
Penina's hand and crossed her own hands over her
chest.

"Mom," said Mom, "you don't get pneumonia from
the cold. You get pneumonia from germs, microbes.
So, being out in the cold, fresh air is actually one of
the *least* likely ways to contract pneumonia."

That was news to Penina. "Then how come you
always tell me to wear my boots, so I don't get double pneumonia?" she asked.

"Because that's what I taught her, darling," Grandma
said. She steered Penina over to the kitchen table.
"Sit down. I'll get you a snack. You're probably
starved."

Penina was kind of hungry, but mostly she was . . .
something. Penina didn't know what to call it. What
do you call it when you won't see your best friend
for a week or your best teacher forever and you're
cold and no one lets you say anything, even when
they ask you a direct question?

"Do you want cocoa? I'll make you some cocoa,"
said Grandma. She opened the refrigerator and

looked inside. "Oh, soy milk. Don't you drink regular milk anymore?"

"There's cow's milk in there, too. Look in the door," said Mom.

"Oh, here it is. Good. For a minute, I thought you were going vegetarian again. Penina, did you know your mother was a vegetarian when she was a teenager? No meat, no chicken, not even eggs or milk. Drove Grandpa and me crazy. She kept that up for about six weeks."

"It was more like a year, Mom."

"Really?" Penina said. She had no idea her mother had been a vegetarian. "Why were you a vegetarian?"

"Oh, I don't know," said Mom. "I was young and foolish, I guess,"

"Your mother was in favor of animal rights," said Grandma.

"Mrs. Brown was, too," said Penina. "I mean, she still is. A vegetarian, that is."

"Well, then, she'll feel right at home in California, I guess," Mom said. She picked up a food-processor attachment thingy and clicked it onto the machine.

"Arizona!" Penina shouted.

"Who's Mrs. Brown?" said Grandma.

"Penina's former teacher," said Mom. "She's moving out west someplace."

"To Arizona!" said Penina. "I told you that. I gave

you Dr. Tobin's letter about that. Come on! Can't you ever pay attention to anything I ever say? Ever?" Penina's voice had gotten high and squeaky and—surprise, surprise—she was crying again. She grabbed a napkin from the napkin holder in the center of the table and used it to wipe her nose.

"Use a tissue, please," Mom suggested. She pushed the tissue box toward Penina.

Penina grabbed it and threw it on the floor. And stomped on it.

"Forget it. I don't want a tissue. Or cocoa. Or latkes. Or anything from you!" Penina screamed. Her throat hurt from screaming. Maybe she really was going to get double pneumonia.

"Penina," said Mom, "calm down. What's wrong with you?" She picked up a potato and the peeler and peeled off a long loop of skin. "I'm sorry, Mom. She's not usually like this. I think she's just upset about her teacher."

Hello! I can hear you!

"You don't need to apologize to me, Sonia. I know what Penina is like, and I know someone else who was just as excitable when she was a little girl."

"Why are you talking about me like I'm not even in the room? I'm standing right here!" Penina yelled. She kicked the tissue box to prove it.

Mom put down the potato and picked up the

tissue box. She placed it neatly on the table. "I was not just like that," she said to Grandma. "I never kicked things."

"No, you kicked people. And I had the bruises to show for it."

"That was an accident! And I was three! Are you ever going to let that go, Mom?"

"Okay. It's gone. I'll never mention it again. I don't need to. Now you're a mother. You know what it's like. When Penina gives you *tsuris*, remember: She's not just my granddaughter. She's my revenge."

Tsuris? Trouble? How had Penina been giving anybody *tsuris*? All she wanted was for people to remember the difference between Arizona and California. "Haven't you ever seen a map? Arizona and California are two separate states! Why don't you look it up online?"

"That's no way to talk to your mother," Dad said. Penina hadn't even seen him come in. "Apologize to her. Now." No *welcome home,* no *how nice to see you,* just a demand that she apologize.

"No! Tell *her* to apologize. I don't need to. I'm just doing my job. Didn't you know that? I'm here to bring you *tsuris*. I'm Grandma's *revenge!*"

The gasps all around almost made Penina feel like someone had finally heard her. Dad gasped. Grandma gasped. Mom gasped. Then she sputtered and pointed at Penina and spit out some growly whispers that ended up with a command that Penina go up to her room.

And stay there.

16. Bad Daughters

Grounded. On Hanukkah.

How was that even possible? Wasn't there some kind of Jewish law against punishing children during times of celebration?

There should be.

How could they do this to her? Were they just going to have Hanukkah without her? Were they going to open presents, eat latkes, play dreidel, sing songs, and light the menorah together while Penina sat upstairs, alone?

Well, not totally alone. She had Daisy. "I love you, Daisy," Penina said. "You're the only one I love."

"Prrt," said Daisy, or something like that.

Penina rubbed the cat's head and cheeks.

Daisy opened her eyes and twitched her ears. She stared accusingly at the door, then leaped off the bed and hid underneath it.

"Can I come in, Penina? I brought you some cocoa," said Grandma.

Of course, she was already in Penina's room when she said it. Naturally, no one ever knocked. Penina was grounded—she was a prisoner. You didn't knock before entering a prison cell, did you?

Grandma put the mug of cocoa on Penina's messy desk. It was Dad's special Penn State mug. She pulled out the desk chair and sat down. "Penina, darling," she said, "I think I owe you an apology."

You sure do, Penina thought. She didn't say it, though. She didn't say anything.

"That *tsimmis* downstairs—that mess—it should have been between your mother and me. We should never have involved you in that. I'm sorry."

Well, okay, it was an apology. It was actually a pretty nice apology, but it was 100 percent for the wrong thing. Penina didn't mind if her mom and grandma had a *tsimmis*. She didn't even mind being in the middle of it. What she did mind was finding out—suddenly and brutally—what her grandma really thought of her. When Penina thought of it, her nose clogged up, and her eyes burned and overflowed. "I'm not just your granddaughter, I'm your *revenge*?"

Grandma smacked herself on the forehead. "I know! What a thing to say. What kind of grand-mother says that?"

Penina's grandmother, apparently. The kind of grandmother who thought Penina was a plague, a

105

punishment, a proof that bad daughters grew up to *have* bad daughters.

Penina needed a tissue, but they were way over there on her desk, near Grandma. Forget it. She wasn't going over there, no matter how much her nose was dripping. She snuffled it in instead.

Grandma got up and brought the tissues with her, the cocoa, too. "Here you go, darling."

Penina blew her nose. She drank some cocoa. It was pretty good. Extra chocolaty, in fact. It even had a marshmallow in it. That was Grandma's touch. Mom never put marshmallows in.

"Have you heard the one about grandparents and grandchildren?" said Grandma. "The reason they have such a special bond?"

"No."

"It's because they share a common enemy!" said Grandma, and laughed at her own joke.

Penina did not think that was funny. Well, maybe just a little bit funny.

"I see a smile," said Grandma. "Oh, how I love that smile. Your hair and eyes come from your father's side of the family, but that smile you get from me."

Penina looked at Grandma's smile. It did look kind of familiar. Maybe she had one like it. But without the peony-pink lipstick.

"Your mother and I have issues. It's been that way

106

ever since she was a little girl. When she was a tod-
dler, she used to scream at me till she was blue in
the face. That's not just an expression. She did it,
screamed herself blue."

It wasn't that hard to picture. Mom didn't scream
herself blue anymore. As a matter of fact, she hardly
ever screamed, but she did get very *determined*. (Like,
for instance, with this grounding thing.) Penina
could imagine Mom at age two, deciding to
scream—and screaming.

"And you know what *my* mother said when

she saw how things were between me and Sonia?"

"What?"

"She said, 'That's my revenge.'"

Penina's hands were freezing. She wrapped them around the Penn State mug. "So, I guess you were a bad daughter, too?" she said. "And having my mother was *your* punishment, and now I'm *her* punishment?" It seemed like a pretty lousy family tradition to Penina.

"Oh, darling! No!" said Grandma. "That's not what I meant. You're not a punishment. You're a prize. You're my dividend, my dessert!" Grandma gave Penina a big squeeze, and she either bumped the cocoa mug or made Penina bump it, because Penina felt a slosh of warm cocoa on her hands and lap.

It didn't hurt—it wasn't hot enough to burn her—but it startled her, so she jumped and spilled the rest of the cocoa on her socks and bedspread and pillowcase, and a little bit on Grandma.

In all the mopping and changing and folding and sorting, Penina never got a chance to ask Grandma anything else about mothers and daughters and revenge and dessert.

"You're no longer grounded, darling," said Grandma. "I got Sonia to commute your sentence. There are still lots of latkes left. Come on down and I'll fix you a plate."

The latkes were hot and greasy and crunchy. Penina ate five, and when she was full, she leaned back in her seat and sighed.

"Feeling better, honey?" Mom asked, refilling Penina's glass of milk—cow's milk.

"Yeah," Penina answered.

"I always say," said Grandma, "there's no problem so big that it can't be solved by a glass of cold milk and a hot potato pancake."

Penina thought there just might be one or two things a potato pancake couldn't solve, but that didn't matter right now. For now she was ready to forget about the *tsimmis* and just enjoy Hanukkah. Grandma and Grandpa passed out the gifts they'd brought with them from the relatives back in Peekskill. Penina got a beautiful blank notebook from Cousin Naomi. Penina liked it a lot. The pages were extra-thick, cream-colored paper, and the cover was smooth, matte black. She ruffled the pages with her thumb.

But instead of the soft paper-flipping sound, Penina heard a squeal and a thump and a roar like an engine revving up. Everyone dropped their presents and boxes and ribbons and wrapping and ran to look out the front window.

17. Jazzy, Snazzy, Zingy

At first, all Penina could see were the Hanukkah menorahs reflected in the windows. But she leaned her forehead against the window, cupped her hands around her face, and watched Zozo's SUV slide across the road. It straightened up, drove backward into Penina's driveway, then forward again, past Penina's house, up the hill, and out in the direction of the main road.

"Where in the world is Vicki going in this weather?" said Mom.

"Aruba," said Penina. "I hope they'll be okay."

Grandma put her arm around Penina, "Don't worry. They will be fine. Did you see that monstrosity they were driving?"

"Uh-huh."

"That's what explorers drive to go over the Himalayas. That kind of SUV can get through the snow and ice on Mt. Everest. Getting to Pittsburgh International Airport won't be a problem."

110

Penina knew Grandma was completely lying. She appreciated the effort.

"Why is Zozo going to the airport?" yelled Mimsy. "Where is Aruba? Can we go with her? When is Zozo coming back?"

Penina felt like throwing something at Mimsy, something soft, nothing that would hurt her, just something to make her shut up. Mimsy's questions were annoying and stupid. And they were embarrassing because Mimsy was shouting out loud the questions Penina was asking silently in her head.

But Penina didn't throw anything at her sister. She handed Mimsy a flat, rectangular box, wrapped in gold foil with a green leafy pattern. It was one of the presents Grandma and Grandpa had brought from Aunt Ethel in Peekskill. Penina got one, too. She shook it. It sounded like a sweater.

And that's what it was. She liked it. It was white and fuzzy and just a little too big, so she could sneak her hands up into the sleeves and keep them warm. Mom and Dad and Mimsy got sweaters, too. Aunt Ethel liked to knit.

Vroom! It was the engine sound again, and a skidding sound, and the sound of everyone stampeding to the front window to see what was up this time.

Penina didn't go to the window. She went right through the front door, grabbing her boots on the way out. The snow had drifted up onto the porch, and Penina hopped around in the snow, pulling on her boots and trying to see inside Zozo's SUV's tinted windows.

Zozo's SUV was parked crossways in Zozo's driveway, windshield wipers and headlights and brake lights all going. The engine cut off and, for a second, everything was silent.

Then the back door opened and Zozo jumped out, and a cheerful, brassy version of "Deck the Halls" blasted from the SUV's sound system.

Penina ran, and Zozo ran, and they met in the knee-high snow drift between their front yards. "You're back!" yelled Penina.

"We're back!" yelled Zozo, "but only until it stops snowing and they plow the roads. As soon as we can, we're going to Aruba."

That was fine with Penina. She hugged her friend. It might not stop snowing for days, and after that, it could be days more before they got the roads clear. She'd have plenty of time to play with Zozo. It was going to be a wonderful vacation.

"Penina, where's your coat? It's freezing out here. You're going to get double pneumonia," said Mrs. Miller.

It wasn't the cold that caused pneumonia. It was

microbes, but Penina didn't clue Mrs. Miller in. She gave Zozo one more welcome-back squeeze, said goodnight, and ran back inside.

She brushed her teeth, put on her pajamas, said goodnight to her parents and grandparents, and went to bed. It was dark, but it wasn't late. Penina was going to bed early, almost as early as Mimsy. The sooner she went to sleep, the sooner she'd wake up tomorrow and call Zozo on the Window Phone.

Penina wasn't tired. She was wide awake. She stared at the ceiling for a while, then stared at the wall. Then she flipped over and stared at the other wall. She coaxed Daisy out from under the bed and tried to get her to cuddle up, but Daisy wasn't cooperating.

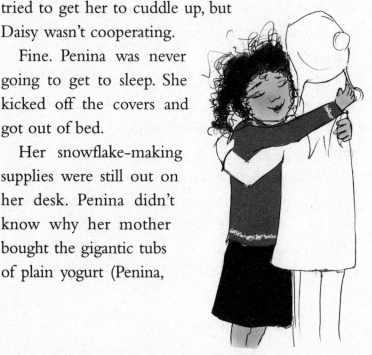

Fine. Penina was never going to get to sleep. She kicked off the covers and got out of bed.

Her snowflake-making supplies were still out on her desk. Penina didn't know why her mother bought the gigantic tubs of plain yogurt (Penina, for one, had never eaten any), but it was a good thing she did, because the lids were good for tracing circles.

Penina put the big, round lid in the middle of a piece of printer paper. She traced around it with her best gel pen and cut on the line. She had a paper circle the size of a gigantic-yogurt-tub lid. She folded the circle in half, then in thirds. Then she started cutting. She'd done so many of these the night before, she didn't even have to think about what she was doing. It was practically automatic.

Penina cut out spikes and curlicues and stair-step patterns, and when she opened the paper back up, she had a pretty paper Jewish star. Well, it was supposed to be a snowflake, but it looked kind of like a six-pointed star, the Star of David, the symbol of Judaism.

Grandma and Grandpa would like that. Penina made another large snowflake and decorated the pair with blue and silver glitter glue. They'd be dry by morning.

Penina yawned. If she went back to bed now, she probably could fall asleep, but she still had one more present to make. She traced another yogurt-lid circle, folded it, but when she cut this one, she made all her cuts in the shape of the letter Z. Z for Zozo.

Zozo was lucky to have such a buzzy name, with such a zig-zaggy first letter.

The snowflake looked great, and covered with gold and silver glitter glue, it looked even better— jazzy, snazzy, zingy, zzzingy.

Penina yawned again. Was *zingy* even a word? She'd ask Zozo in the morning. In the morning, Zozo would be here, not in Aruba. She'd be right next door, where she belonged.

18. Quack Quack

"I love it! Thank you!" said Zozo.

"It's beautiful, darling, just like you," said Grandma.

"Thank you, Penina. I'll put it up in my office where I can see it every day, and I'll think of you every time I look at it," said Grandpa.

They all held up their glittery, shimmery, festive paper snowflakes and grinned at one another.

"You're welcome," said Penina. She looked down and played with a piece of wrinkled wrapping paper. It was a little embarrassing, this massive gratitude rush.

Mrs. Miller oohed and ahhed over the snowflake Penina had made for Zozo, and Penina wished she'd made one for her, too. Zozo and her mom were spending the day at Penina's house. And maybe the evening, and maybe the next day. The snow had stopped that morning, but the roads wouldn't be clear for a while.

"Penina," said Mrs. Miller, "what's it called, again? Doodle?"

"What?"

"The top, what's it called?"

Penina had no idea what Mrs. Miller was talking about. She looked at Zozo for help, but Zozo was talking to Grandma.

"Dreidel!" yelled Mimsy. "It's a dreidel!"

Oh, yeah. That's what Mrs. Miller meant. The dreidel was a spinning top, and playing it was a Hanukkah tradition. Mrs. Greenbaum always gave them colorful plastic dreidels to play with at the religious school Hanukkah party, and Penina had collected a lot of them over the years. "I'll be right back!" she yelled.

She ran up the stairs, got her box of dreidels, ran back downstairs, and dumped the box out on the coffee table. Dozens of plastic dreidels—blue, green, pink, orange, white, purple—rolled across the wood and dropped off the edges.

"I get to be pink!" yelled Mimsy, which was stupid, because, first of all, there were about four pink dreidels, plenty to go around, and second of all, that wasn't how you played dreidel anyhow. You didn't get to "be" a color. You just spun it.

"I get the red one," said Zozo.

117

Grandma wanted white. Grandpa picked blue. Mom and Dad got orange and yellow, and Mrs. Miller picked purple. Penina grabbed a green one.

"Mimsy dear, bring me my bag," Grandma said. Mimsy did, and Grandma reached in and took out three rolls of pennies. "Here you go, girls, let me stake your first round. You can pay me back out of your winnings." She placed a roll of pennies on Mimsy's upturned hand. Then Penina's, then Zozo's.

"Thank you, ma'am," Zozo said.

"Ma'am? Oh, please! Call me Trudy," said Grand-

ma. "Now, everybody put a penny in the kitty!"

The kitty was the pile of coins in the middle of the table. Penina didn't know why Grandma called it that, but she always had.

"Let's make this interesting," said Mrs. Miller. "I'm in for a nickel." She gave her purple dreidel a spin, and it twirled, twirled, twirled so fast it looked like it was standing still.

It fell, and everyone leaned in to see which side had landed up.

"*Gimmel!*" said Mimsy.

Gimmel was the best letter on the dreidel. It meant "take all." There were four sides, four letters: *nun, gimmel, hay,* and *shin.* Each letter meant something different.

"No, sweetie, that's not a *gimmel,* that's a *nun.* See? No tail," said Mom.

The letter *nun* looked a lot like *gimmel,* but the *gimmel* had a little extra part to it. It really did look like a tail.

"So, is that good?" asked Mrs. Miller. "What does that mean?"

"Nothing," said Grandpa.

"It doesn't mean anything?"

"*Nun* means do nothing. You don't get any coins, but you don't have to put any in, either," said Grandma. "Zozo, it's up to you."

Zozo spun like a pro. Her dreidel went for a long time and finally landed on *hay.*

"Take half, you lucky ducky," Penina said.

"Quack quack!" said Zozo, triumphantly scooping up half the pile of coins. That cracked them both up.

"Me next!" yelled Mimsy. She did something to her fluorescent pink dreidel, and it skidded off the edge of the table. Mimsy swooped down and got it. "*Gimmel!*" she shouted.

"That doesn't count," Penina said. "It has to be on the table."

"It does so count!"

"But you picked it up before anyone could see it!" said Penina.

"So?" Mimsy said.

"I'm sure if Mimsy says she got a *gimmel*, she got a *gimmel*," said Mom. "You're next, Penina. Maybe you'll get a *gimmel*, too."

Penina didn't want a *gimmel*. She didn't want any letter. She didn't want anything to do with this game.

But Zozo caught her eye and made a face like, *so Mimsy cheats, who cares?* And Grandma said, "The green dreidel is the lucky one. Let's see what you get." So Penina decided to keep playing. She gave the dreidel a good spin, and she held her breath while it twirled around.

"*Shin!*" yelled Mimsy, when the dreidel fell. "Put one in!"

Penina frowned at the dreidel. It was a *shin*. She dropped one of her pennies into the kitty. Maybe for her next turn she'd borrow Zozo's red dreidel. It was a lucky one.

Mom got a *shin*, too. That made Penina feel better. Maybe it shouldn't, but it did. Then Dad got a *shin*, and so did Grandpa. They all smiled at each other like, *just our luck, huh?* By the time it was Grandma's turn, there was a lot of money in the kitty.

Grandma kissed her dreidel. "Come on, *gimmel*," she said. She gave it a twirl, and it was a good one. That dreidel spun for about a minute, which, when you're waiting for a dreidel to drop, is a long time.

"*Gimmel!*" shouted Grandpa. "How do you do it, Trudy? I don't think I've ever seen you get anything worse than a *hay*."

Grandma patted Grandpa's arm. "Some secrets I cannot reveal, even to you, my darling," she said. She scooped the pile of coins toward her and arranged them into little towers.

She must have had some kind of secret, or just incredible luck, because they played five more rounds, and Grandma got *gimmel, gimmel, hay, gimmel, hay*. By then, Penina, Mom, and Grandpa were out of coins. Everyone else was getting tired of playing.

"Back home," said Grandma, "in the market where I shop, they have an interesting contraption. It's a big plastic funnel. You drop a coin along the edge, and it circles around and around the funnel before falling through the hole. It's fun to watch, and it raises money for the animal shelter. Do they have anything like that here?"

"Yes—" Penina started to answer.

"At the library!" Mimsy cut her off. "To buy new books."

"Good," said Grandma. "Then take these coins, and next time you go to the library, I want you to put them in the funnel for me, okay?" She gave Mimsy some of her coins, but she kept some back and gave them to Penina and Zozo, too.

"Hey watch!" said Zozo. She held the change in her hands, with her palms up and her pinky fingers side by side. She tossed the coins up into the air, pizza-dough style, and caught them on the backs of her hands.

"Me, too!" yelled Mimsy. She tried it, but the coins just sort of rained down all around her and rolled all over the place. "No fair!" she shouted.

But for once, no one paid attention to her. They were all trying the coin-flip trick, dropping coins, chasing them, trying again. Penina got so she could flip a small fortune without dropping more than three or four cents.

Finally, Mom came in with the *tzedakah* box. It always made Penina think of a cookie tin because it was made of the same type of painted metal. But it was smaller and covered in pictures of trees and vines and flowers.

"We'll put it with the library books," said Mom, "and we'll take it with us next time we go."

Everyone poured their pennies into the box. It was noisy, but in a nice way. Then Grandpa put something in, but it didn't make any noise. Paper money?

He winked at Penina like, *that's just between you and me, okay?*

Okay, Penina winked back.

"It's getting dark," said Dad, "time to light the menorah."

Mimsy ran to the front window and began filling her menorah with candles. Every single one of them needed a big, huge explanation about how it ranked in the list of Mimsy's favorite colors and why she was putting it in and whether or not it was the *shamash*.

Penina took her menorah and her box of candles and brought them to Zozo. "Here," Penina said, "you can pick the colors."

Zozo took them. "Wow, this thing is heavy," she said, hefting the menorah. "Does it matter which colors I use?"

"No, just make it pretty."

"Okay." Zozo put the menorah on the coffee table and started pulling candles from the box. "Don't look. I'll tell you when I'm done."

"Oh, pardon me, Miss Secret Mysterious Candle Design," Penina said, but she turned her back while Zozo filled the menorah.

124

"Ta-da!" sang Zozo. "Turn around!"

Red, green, red, green, red, green, red, and a white *shamash*. Penina's little menorah was done up in Christmas colors. "Cute," Penina said.

"It's our favorite colors," Zozo said. "My favorite color is red, and yours is green, right?"

"Oh, yeah."

"And the white one is just because I ran out of red and green, and I thought it looked good. I could put a blue one in instead."

"No, it looks nice."

And it looked even better in the window with the big menorah and Mimsy's little one.

Grandma, Grandpa, Mom, Dad, Mimsy, and Penina all said the blessing together.

"Ve-tzivanu le-hadlik ner shel Hanukkah."

They sounded good, really good. Penina thought that if the singing family from *The Sound of Music* ever sang the Hanukkah blessing, this is how they would sound.

But Grandpa kept singing. There were two or three verses to the Hanukkah blessing, even though Penina's family usually just sang the first one. Grandpa had a really nice voice. He probably could have been an opera singer if he hadn't decided to be a pharmacist. He made the blessing sound like something old and serious, something that could have

125

echoed through a ruined temple and rededicated it for Jewish prayer. Which, Penina supposed, is how the blessing was supposed to sound.

"Bayamim hahem bazman hazeh."

Penina stared at the brilliant, glittering, sparkling, glowing, dancing Hanukkah lights. Mimsy came over and leaned against her, and Penina didn't even knock her away.

"Do you mind if I put on the news, just for a minute?" Mrs. Miller said. "I want to hear an update on the roads."

"Of course," said Mom, "come on into the den."

They disappeared into the den for a minute, then Mrs. Miller came whooping back out. She hugged Zozo and picked her up and whirled her around. "Come on, Zoze! Get your coat. The roads are clear! We're going to Aruba!"

19. Socks and Underwear

"What was that book where the kid wished it could be Christmas every day?" said Penina.

"Um, *Little House in the Big Woods?*" said Mom. Penina could tell she was just picking names out of the air. She had no idea what Penina was talking about.

"No," Penina said, "it wasn't that. The girl in this book wanted it to be Christmas every day. Once she got her wish, she found out she didn't like it." Penina felt like that girl, except with Hanukkah instead of Christmas. Eight days was enough. She couldn't eat one more latke. She couldn't spin one more dreidel. She couldn't open one more present.

Well, she might be able to open another present. There were still a few packages left. Everyone was sitting around in the living room, pretty much covered by scraps of wrapping paper, ribbons, gift boxes, and packing peanuts. The menorahs were blazing away in the front window. Three menorahs, nine lights each: twenty-seven lights. Once they'd burned down, that was it until next year.

"I've always loved that book," Mom sighed. "In a couple of years, when Mimsy is old enough, I can read it to her."

"I'm old enough! Read it now, Mommy!" Mimsy demanded. She didn't seem to be too clued in to what they were talking about, though, because she picked up some other book, a book about ballerinas or something, and shoved it at Mom. Mom snuggled Mimsy onto her lap and began reading softly.

"Hey, Penina," whispered Grandma, "what does that package say, the flat silver one over there?"

Penina grabbed it and checked the tag. "It says, 'to Penina, from Grandma and Grandpa,'" Penina reported.

"Open it up," Grandma said.

Penina tapped on the package. It was weighty and solid. Probably a book, a big one. She tore off the paper. That's what it was. It had a deep red cover with gold decorations and fancy gold lettering. Penina read the title, *"The Annotated Alice."*

The Annotated Alice? As in, *Alice in Wonderland?* Penina had seen the movie, a cartoon about a girl stuck in a crazy nonsense magical land. It was confusing and not very funny. "Thanks, Grandma. Thanks, Grandpa," Penina said. Oh well, she'd gotten lots of other nice gifts. It didn't matter that this one was a dud.

"Come here, Penina-leh," said Grandma. Penina brought the book and stood by Grandma's chair. "Do you know what *annotated* means?"

As a matter of fact, Penina did not know what *annotated* meant, but she didn't know if she should say so. She squinted at the book. She didn't want to admit to Grandma that she couldn't even understand her Hanukkah gift. "It means unedited," Penina said, "like, this is the whole book, not cut down for children." It seemed like a good guess to her.

"Good guess," said Grandma. "*Annotated* just means that it has notes. This is *Alice's Adventures in Wonderland* and *Through the Looking Glass*, together with notes explaining the stories."

"Wow. Thanks," Penina said. She guessed this was almost as good as getting socks and underwear.

Grandma chuckled and gently tugged a little bit of Penina's hair. "It's not that bad, darling."

Penina hadn't meant to be ungrateful. It was a really nice book. It was just, kind of, not very interesting.

But Grandma didn't look offended. She was

actually laughing a little. "We got it for you because we hear you're a real math *maven*."

"Really?" Who had told her that? And what did that have to do with *The Annotated Alice*?

"Yes, of course. The Alice books are full of mathematical puzzles and jokes. Lewis Carroll was really a professor of mathematics at Cambridge University in England."

"Oxford," said Grandpa.

"I meant Oxford," said Grandma. "The stories aren't just nonsense. They're all about logic and probability and set theory."

"And imaginary numbers?" asked Penina.

"Naturally," said Grandma. "And there's something else. Look at this." She took the book from Penina and paged through it a little. "Here." She pointed at a poem in the middle of the book. What's that say?"

Penina read the word above Grandma's neat, trim fingernail. "Mimsy," she said. She couldn't help groaning a little. So Mimsy's name was in a book. Big deal. What was so great about having your name in a book, anyhow? And why make a big, huge point of showing it to her?

"What's it mean?" asked Grandma, like this was some kind of delicious joke she and Penina were in on together. Grandma was crazy.

Penina rolled her eyes. "It's a nickname for Miriam. Why don't you ask my mom why she picked it. I have no idea."

"That's not what it means here," said Grandma. "Read the note." She pointed to the smaller type along the side of the page, the annotations.

Penina read. She couldn't believe it, so she reread. "It means *miserable* or *contemptible*," she said. She was grinning. She couldn't help it. It was pretty funny.

"I thought you'd get a kick out of that," said Grandma.

"Out of what?" yelled Mimsy.

"Nothing," Penina said. Mimsy had been less annoying than usual all day, and Penina didn't want to get her all stirred up. Making fun of her name would only make Mimsy scream and cry and tattle, and that would make Penina grounded for the whole rest of vacation.

"Why were you laughing?" Mimsy yelled. "What is that?" She tried to grab the book from Penina, but Penina had a height advantage.

"It's a book, from Grandma and Grandpa," said Penina. "And it has your name in it, look."

"Penina," said Mom. That was all she said, just Penina's name, but it was as if she'd said, *Penina, don't you dare say anything mean about Mimsy's name.*

131

Don't you dare say anything mean about Mimsy—or to Mimsy—ever.

Mom didn't need to tell her that. Penina gave Mom a look: *I am being nice to her.*

She crouched down to show Mimsy the book. "See, what's that say?" Mimsy couldn't read much, but she knew what her name looked like.

"You read it," said Mimsy. She was probably used to bigger letters, and not in italics.

"Look at it letter by letter," said Penina. She pointed at each one. "M–I–M–S–Y."

"Mimsy!" said Mimsy. "That's my name!" She tore off through the drifts of wrapping paper and ribbons, singing her name over and over, occasionally reminding everyone that it was in a book.

"Good save," whispered Grandma.

"You could be a teacher," said Dad. "I like the way you helped Mimsy read her name."

"And how you glossed over the definition," said Grandpa.

Mom came over and squeezed Penina around the shoulders. "That was nice of you, Penina. You're a good big sister."

Mom was wearing her fluffy sweater from Aunt Ethel. It was like Mrs. Brown's sweater, but white and kind of baggy. Penina put her arm around Mom. The sweater felt soft and fuzzy. Penina leaned her head on her mother. That felt nice, too.

20. Happy New Year!

Dear Mrs. Brown,

Happy New Year!

How's the weather in Tucson?

We got 6 inches of snow, and it's 30 degrees out (22 degrees with the wind chill.) I bet you don't miss that!

Zozo came back from Aruba and brought some beautiful seashells. She says she had a wonderful time, even if she didn't get to swim with dolphins.

Here's a picture of Zozo and Anne and Jackie and me on New Year's Eve. We had a sleepover at Zozo's house. We toasted the new year with fake champagne (sparkling grape juice). We drank a toast to you, too. We miss you already.

Zozo and Anne and Jackie say hi (especially Zozo). Please tell your sister hi for us, too.

We all hope she's feeling better soon.

School starts again in a couple of days. I wonder what our new teacher will be like. Even if she's really really really nice, she'll never be as good a teacher as you.

My new year's resolution is to get all As in math, and to read the whole <u>Annotated Alice.</u> I got it for Hanukkah, and it's really good. Did you know that Lewis Carroll was a teacher?

Wishing you a frabjous New Year. ("Frabjous" is from Alice. It means "fabulous" and "joyous.")

Your student,
Penina Levine

Who will be Penina's new teacher?
What will she try to make Penina do?
Why will Penina refuse?
How will Penina explain to Zozo why she's grounded, again?

Find out in

Penina Levine Is a Hard-Boiled Egg,

available now.